Minnie Santangelo and The Evil Eye

By Anthony Mancini

MINNIE SANTANGELO'S MORTAL SIN
MINNIE SANTANGELO AND THE EVIL EYE

MINNIE SANTANGELO & THE EVIL EYE

Anthony Mancini

Coward, McCann & Geoghegan, Inc.   New York

Copyright © 1977 by Anthony Mancini

All rights reserved. This book, or parts thereof, may not be reproduced in any form without permission in writing from the publisher. Published on the same day in Canada by Longman Canada Limited, Toronto.

SBN: 698-10818-3

Library of Congress Cataloging in Publication Data

Mancini, Anthony.
 Minnie Santangelo and the evil eye.

 I. Title.
PZ4.M269Mh3   [PS3563.A4354]   813'.5'4   77-4494

Printed in the United States of America

Lovingly dedicated to my father Ugo,
a strong family man.

What was that snaky-headed, Gorgon shield that wise Minerva wore . . . ?

—John Milton

Part One
The Baptism

Chapter 1

On the way to midnight mass the villagers heard the bleat of the shepherds' bagpipes drifting down the hills with the fog. They tramped through the vapor thick upon the patient countryside toward the old church that stood at the pinnacle of the village at the end of a winding road. To the skirl of the pipes, some of the peasants sang a Christmas song about a divine child descending from heaven. But others whispered behind cupped hands the litany of a far more ancient religion.

Montevecchio. A whitewashed hive of creviced stone and plaster in the region of Campania. Here, olive groves clung to rocky slopes as the people kept a precarious hold on life. Here, the people, grudging as the soil itself, paid unremitting tribute to the State, the Church, and history. Yet in their heart of hearts they kept another faith.

It was 1935. The young men of Montevecchio had been conscripted by the State to die in Ethiopia and drafted by history to toil in the construction gangs of America. The women stayed to combat older enemies.

The afflicted girl lived on the Viale della Sorgente not far from the main square. Her whimpers escaped through the French doors leading to the bedroom. She lay flat on her back, one hand on her swollen belly, the other gripping her husband's hand. He was on military leave. Her mother and younger brother stood close by, their faces portraits of stoicism in the glow of the oil lamp. They watched the pregnant girl thrashing her head in pain on a perspiration-stained pillow. Her russet curls, the color of winter apples, framed aristocratic features and green eyes. She was a beautiful girl to whom even pain was becoming. Her looks, social class, and good marriage had made her the envy of the other village girls. Now she suffered this strange illness. They feared the worst.

The peasants called Simonetta "the gifted woman." She was old and wrinkled like a dried fig, but she carried herself with strength and dignity past the worshippers filing into church. Eva the serving girl gave Simonetta a deferential sidelong look and beckoned her to follow. She nodded. There was work to be done.

As healer, as white witch, Simonetta played a major role in village affairs. She was considered more important—though she acted less self-important—even than the Fascist mayor or the regional tax collector. She walked straight ahead, her eyes fixed on a point in space, following Eva's lead. The villagers formed murmuring clusters in her wake while the pastor frowned out into the fog mantling the church steps.

Pigs, chickens, and goats sounded a dissonant chorus in the night. Fires blazed on hearths and smoke wafted from chimneys as Christmas Eve dinners of spaghetti and roast squab simmered. Led by the serving girl, Simonetta went down into the village.

The healer was tall and stooped, with the linear grace of an aquatic bird. She seemed an apparition, walking through the strands of fog gathering over the square where the fountain gurgled. She wore a black veil tumbling to her shoulders in folds, a muslin blouse, and long, wide skirt.

Arriving at the wooden door to a two-story house with a balcony, a structure much finer than the peasants' shacks surrounding it, Simonetta paused under the goat's horns hung over the threshhold as an amulet. The serving girl shoved the door open with her shoulder and stood aside, waiting for the witch woman to enter. A mule brayed in the yard, as she followed her indoors. They passed through a large room with tile flooring and gray plaster walls, and went up the stairs.

In the sick girl's room the family waited. The mother stood with arms folded and expression resigned. She wore the black, lace-trimmed finery of the landowning class. The man, barely twenty-one with a stubby mustache and darting black eyes, still gripped his wife's moist hand.

The witch woman greeted them with an economical incline of the head and looked down at the suffering girl, whose copper skin was discolored like a moldering penny. Her brow sizzled at the touch of Simonetta's hand.

The healer asked the family routine questions about the history of the illness. They told her the girl had first complained of headaches and that when they got worse and she grew feverish they had summoned a doctor from Naples. He suspected malaria and prescribed quinine. She had not responded to the drug. The doctor, of whom the family became more and more suspicious, was baffled. He was the sort who masked his ignorance with optimism, so he told them there was nothing seriously wrong.

Day by day, her strength ebbed and her color failed. She was six months pregnant but the illness did not seem connected to her condition—at least not physically. As her health continued to deteriorate, the family decided to seek help from another source of knowledge and power.

Simonetta then turned to recent family history. From the girl's mother she learned that the couple had been married eight months before in a splendid ceremony that had been the talk of the village. She spared Simonetta no details—the food, the music, the tributes paid the family and the couple—all were minutely catalogued to show Simonetta who lived in the hills with the wolves and wild boars how important and prosperous the family was. The witch woman listened closely, without a single interruption. Her marble eyes seemed never to blink.

The girl's father, now dead, had been an army colonel who had once been Montevecchio's mayor. The girl's husband came from an equally prominent family in a neighboring village. When she quickly became pregnant after the marriage, the couple's good fortune seemed sealed. She and her situation had been praised lavishly and with undertones of envy by many of the women of Montevecchio.

The healer frowned now and touched the bag of garlic hanging around the feverish young girl's neck.

She questioned the young husband closely about any relationships he might have had before his betrothal. He admitted he had courted a girl in his own village for a short time before their families had quarreled and broken it off. Had the first girl been angry and had she ever gazed upon his wife? The young man said no, but he recalled that the first girl's mother had been furious at the broken engagement. He recalled that she later cooled down and even paid a visit after the wedding, bringing a gift of bed linen. He remembered her praising his wife's beauty and staring at her long and hard.

The healer's face was grim. *All the signs were there.* Yet experience taught her to draw no conclusions before putting it to the test. Further probing revealed that, when the girl was first feeling ill, her mere entry into a room would often cause others to yawn.

Simonetta asked the girl's mother to bring a basin of water and a cruet of olive oil. Gathering up her bell-shaped skirts the mother hurried down to the kitchen, while the brother, a sparrow of a boy, was instructed to close the French doors leading to the balcony. When the mother returned with the water and oil, the white witch was mumbling a *pater noster*. She finished the prayer, took the basin of water and set it on a table. When the sick girl gave a deep growl of pain, her husband's knuckles whitened.

The healer picked up the cruet of oil and poured three drops into the water. The family huddled closer to Simonetta, for a moment forgetting the suffering girl. In the distance, the church bells clanged tinnily.

Simonetta dropped to one knee and blew on the surface of the water. The three little globules of oil stirred. Time came to a dead halt for a fraction of a second as the drops merged to form a single circle like a glaring eye. Then the eye disappeared into the water.

The family shuddered in unison, and the husband looked imploringly at the healer.

"I will try," Simonetta shrugged, promising nothing. "Take off her chemise," she instructed the mother. The white witch then took it down to the kitchen where a fire was built on the hearth. She boiled the chemise in a copper pot, picking at it with a long meat fork, then went back upstairs.

A fresh basin of water was brought into the room and the healer reached into her bodice to produce a Saint Anthony's medal. It glittered with power. She took the religious medal and used it to make the sign of the cross over the afflicted girl three times—each time chanting a *pater noster*. Over the oil and water she performed the same ritual, crossing herself three times and deliberately omitting the *amen*.

She took a teaspoon of olive oil, dipped the medal into it and held the medal above the water. As the drops of oil formed and fell, she chanted, *"Offro 'ste preghiere a beat' eternita—scaccia 'stu malocchio da questa ragazza. Scaccia tutt' infermite e malattie."*

She continued to let oil drip from the medal until the circles in the water got smaller and smaller, the girl's breathing more and more regular. Soon she seemed to be resting peacefully, but Simonetta still did not proclaim victory. How deceptive these encounters could be! The oil in the water glistened now like an armada of tearful eyes. *Eyes.*

The healer took the oil-soaked medal and crossed the girl's forehead with it seven times, repeating the Lord's Prayer. The girl's face was composed, her breathing regular.

The healer added salt to the basin and carried the mixture out through the French doors to the balcony. She poured the liquid over the rusted iron railings into the street.

"*Aqua e sale,*" she sang out, "water and salt. Whatever the envious witch has invented, let it fail, let it fail."

The liquid was sucked up by the parched soil of Montevecchio.

Eyes.

Chapter 2

Minerva Santangelo would describe herself as the mother of a son who was always going off somewhere. She would say this not with a resigned shrug but with a frown. Then her face would soften. While taking the ways of other people, her son had never given up those of his own. Of that she was proud. Besides, if he was always going off somewhere, he was often coming home too, giving her the chance to treat him like the beloved prodigal. He was coming home again tomorrow. So Minnie would also describe herself as very happy.

"Happy" this time was an understatement, even for a woman of Minnie's untethered emotions. This time would be the champagne of her homemade vintage of pleasures, for her son Remo was bringing something special home. *A grandson.*

She felt a little shiver of anticipation as she crossed Mulberry Street. It was July and the tar melted on the roofs of the brick tenements of Little Italy. Minnie walked with the grace of a former peasant girl who once had balanced clay pots on her head. Her hands gripped the twisted handles of two shopping bags full of fresh fruit and vegetables, butcher-shop meats, cheeses, and freshly baked bread—all from the neighborhood, a place where blessings were mixed with blight.

This village within the big city had been home to Minnie since a steamship brought her here from the Abruzzi almost forty years before. At first, she had shed tears at the squalor of the place in contrast to the burnt-umber beauty of her homeland. But soon she grew to love it as she would love practically any place she lived. Minnie had a way of making things her own.

Now she headed for Hester Street. Here as a young widow she had raised her son, suffered more than her share of tragedy, worshipped her God and her saints. Here, she had discovered the pleasures of bingo and soap opera and advice-to-the-lovelorn columns. She made love for the first time here. And she made friends here.

She turned a corner and walked flush into the westering sun, blinking her hazel eyes. She smiled at the slanted stairs of the fire escapes, at the stone, brick, and asphalt of her neighborhood. Minnie had preserved a child's natural acceptance of things and an indomitable hopefulness. Her olive-skinned face reflected stoic optimism. The trash on the streets might have been flowers in a garden, the way she felt. The way she was. Somehow, she had achieved composure, though not at the cost of her fighting spirit. Minnie was clever at such crucial arts as haggling in the local markets, and aware that people had their dark sides. But her first instinct was always to trust. In a way, Minnie Santangelo was a gifted woman.

She had been pretty as a girl. Now she was just pleasant-looking and her figure had puffed out like a breakfast roll. But she still took pride in her appearance and would never leave the apartment in a housedress or with runs in her stockings.

She crossed Grand Street, acknowledging the greetings of neighbors, shopkeepers, and restaurant owners. The shadows of the street lamps were lengthening and Minnie had only the fish store left on her list. She wanted to buy clams for the spaghetti sauce *alle vongole.* Tomorrow Minnie would prepare a feast.

A cat as beautiful as an ebony figurine darted between the trash cans—a black queen incongruous in this shabby setting. Minnie took fleeting notice of her before turning her thoughts to other matters. She followed her sense of smell down the pungent street. Bread, then citrus, then fennel, then fish. At Mario's, she looked over the Little Necks resting on a bed of ice in the front window, entered the store and bought three dozen as well as a small filet for her own dinner that evening.

As she left, she almost collided with a barefoot blond girl dressed in blue jeans and a halter top, and leading a sheep dog on a leash toward Broome Street. An Italian popular song blared from the record-store speakers.

On the way home, Minnie passed the Church of Christ's Passion, a small brick building set back from the street behind a stone wall and a small courtyard. There the hunchback Fortunato Ricci was mixing cement to replace a few bricks on the corner of the building. His expression, as always, was sour as a persimmon, but he mustered a crooked smile for Minnie. "*Salve, Seen-yo,*" he saluted her in his heavy Neapolitan accent, sweating on this humid evening.

Minnie flashed the dwarf a warm smile. "*Ciao*, Fortunato. It's too hot to be working so hard. Why don't you take it easy?"

"Sure," he answered, leaning on his shovel. "I'll drive down to the country club for a dip in the pool."

Her expression changed from sunniness to sympathy "Come on now. Life's not so bad here." Her tone was coaxing. "Why don't you go to a nice air-conditioned movie?"

" 'Cause I don't speak Chinese," he said with a sardonic smile. He mopped his brow with the sleeve of his brown cotton shirt. His cold nature thawed in the warm climate of Minnie's presence. "*Come va, Seen-yo?* How you been? I hear you're going to meet your grandson."

"*Finalmente.*" She raised her eyes to the sky. "He will be baptized next week in Saint Theresa's."

"Good you don't bring him to this insignificant little church."

Minnie frowned. "Fortunato. It is still the house of God."

"When you live here, it doesn't seem so holy. You know, it loses its mystery," he replied with an unrepentant shrug.

Minnie's piety did not stop her from sympathizing. She thought it must not be very pleasant to live alone in a furnished room in the basement of a church. Fortunato Ricci swatted a fly that had alighted on his shoulder. He raised his homely face to her and smiled in cruel triumph. "Got him."

Fortunato was forty years old and exactly four feet tall. His black hair was parted three-quarters of the distance from his left to his right ear and slicked back with baby oil. He looked at a world he found inadequate through eyes that were slightly crossed. His face was intelligent despite all its disadvantages and conveyed the sense of a man who knew, for example, that unexpected things were more likely to occur at night. Minnie and he shared an odd kinship. Fortunato liked her, as he did few people. He was a man who cultivated cynicism, and though he worked in a church, he rang no bells. No soft-hearted Quasimodo he. But Minnie, with her direct and unquestioning nature, got through to him.

She asked, "You will come to the baptism party?"

He frowned. "Thanks, no. You don't want the child to have bad luck, do you?"

She touched his forearm. "I insist you come, Fortunato. All my friends from the neighborhood will be there."

He took up his shovel and swirled the wet cement. "I appreciate the invitation, *Seen-yo.* But I play poker Saturday nights."

"Make an exception. Or go later."

"What do you want me around for? Everybody will have a better time if I don't show my face."

"That's silly. *I* won't have a better time." She pouted.

"Listen, you don't have to decide right this minute. But keep in mind that I will be offended if you don't come. Anyhow, see how you feel about it next week."

Casually he shoveled more sand into the circle of water. "I take my poker seriously, Signora Santangelo."

"I take my friends seriously," she said.

"I'm a good poker player. I don't have much experience with friendship."

"You can learn that too."

Minnie left him still leaning on a shovel that was almost as big as he and went home to her apartment on Hester Street. There were two corner windows in the kitchen of the three-room apartment. There in the kitchen Minnie spent most of her time. From one window hung two flags—the Stars and Stripes and the Italian tricolor. In the other window hung a Swedish ivy plant which Minnie cared for with gruff affection. After she had stored the groceries, she doused the plant with water she always left sitting around in a wine bottle. By all rights, the plant should have been wilting in the humidity, but it seemed healthy enough. The setting sun framed the tenements with pink light. As she looked out the window, Minnie felt depressed without knowing why. Perhaps it was the instinctive melancholy of a woman alone at dusk. She thought about tomorrow's homecoming and what little Stefano would be like. She felt she already knew him from Remo's letters—a placid baby with a grown-up smile. She could visualize him with puckered skin and downy hair. He was six months old and not yet yet baptized, but that didn't worry Minnie. Although she was a good Catholic, she couldn't quite bring herself to believe God would hold anything against an innocent baby just because he wasn't baptized.

The baby was named after Minnie's husband who was killed while on vacation in Sicily many years before. It was the bloody work of a crazy man with hate in his heart. This same man had carried an old family feud across the ocean and laid terror at Minnie's doorstep. Ultimately, she had been forced to deal with it. It was an experience that gave her stature and the outcome made her special in the neighborhood. But for Minnie the whole story was still painful to think about.

Depression lingered like an unwelcome guest. She should have been brimming with pleasant thoughts of tomorrow. She *was* eager, in a subdued way. But something seemed wrong. Minnie had the gift of intuition, and her fifty-seven years had taught her to respect her own forebodings. She knew a sure cure for her melancholia. Cooking.

After she had begun tomorrow's meal, she cooked her own dinner, frying the fish simply in lemon and olive oil and adding a few spices. She ate it with bread, a small salad, and little gusto. Evening merged into night and her mood returned, hanging heavy in the air with the humidity. She scraped her plates into the trash can, stacked them in soapy water, and prepared for bed.

Her bedroom also had a window on the world—a back alley and a small scrap of sky. By midnight, a wind had risen to disperse the moisture and the sky was spattered with stars. Brushing black hair streaked with gray, Minnie looked up at the swath of sky. For no apparent reason, two insignificant experiences of the day surfaced in her memory—glimpsing the slim black cat in the alley, and almost colliding with the barefoot girl with the sheep dog outside the fish store. Flashes of life.

Stroking her hair with distracted sensuality, she looked up again at the effulgent stars. A multitude of eyes stared out through the mask of night.

Chapter 3

The next day Minnie's kitchen was filled with the odor of a magical ingredient. Garlic.

It was in the salad and the spaghetti sauce, in the *broccoli a crudo*, sautéed with wine, in the *bracioline di agnello*, the baby lamp chops of Abruzzi that Minnie's father had taught her to cook. The bulbous lily hung in garlands from an electrical cord over the kitchen doorway, not just as a staple of Minnie's art, but as mystical guarantor of health, sexual vigor, and protection from evil. On this day in Minnie Santangelo's apartment it was working its magic.

It was a Brueghel scene. Arturo Longo, a man with a hang-dog look but goodness etched around the eyes, clinked glasses of gritty Fernet with Ray Santangelo. Aunt Angela Treponti put two manicured fingers coyly to her fleshy cheek and whooped at Doctor Agosto Bevilaqua's naughty story. Sister Anastasia, a melancholic nun, quietly sipped Campari. Ray's wife Cynthia sat off to the side doing needlepoint, while Minnie, waving the wooden spoon that was almost an extension of her arm, gurgled and squeaked energetically to entertain Stefano Santangelo II.

He was exactly as she had imagined him—round and even-tempered, with the alert gray eyes of his father and grandfather. At the moment he was plumped on the living-room rug, studying the contours of an armchair's clawed foot. In his right fist was a wet pretzel. He grinned skillfully at his rapt grandmother. Affection flared like a bonfire.

Cynthia had to smile at the picture they made: the baby holding a pretzel and the grandmother a wooden spoon. Cynthia was beginning to feel less an alien among Ray's people. It had taken about a year for her to start to get used to it all. She cast her eyes down to her needlepoint cushion. She was a pretty woman of bones and planes. A sculpted face, lean jutting hips, long sinewy legs. With the fashion-model figure went slightly aristocratic pretensions. She was the daughter of a Baton Rouge postal clerk and a half-French, Catholic mother whose maiden name was Corbett (originally Courbet). Her father, strapping son of a sharecropper, had met her mother at a dance marathon and made her pregnant the same night. To compensate for her loss of other virtues, the mother held tightly to her southern-belle airs and had passed them along to her only daughter.

Cynthia inherited her looks from her father: red hair worn in sprigs of short curls, outsized brown eyes framed by thick brows she didn't pluck and that lent her a look of perpetual sternness. She spoke with a slight lisp.

All day long, neighborhood women had been coming to pay their respects, cooing over Stefano and introducing themselves to Cynthia with what she regarded as an excess of familiarity. Many of the women, especially Carmela Paoli who lived on Grand Street, were shocked to see Cynthia breast-feed Stefano. They wondered why she had such old-fashioned, lower-class ideas. Bottled formula was *much* healthier for the child—and much more the American way. Minnie, though, was sympathetic to breast-feeding, remembering when she herself and every other mother she knew did it.

"There's nothing like the mother's own milk," she announced to all, "to protect the child. It's healthy, and besides, the breast makes the baby feel safe and warm."

"Makes the mother feel good, too," Cynthia observed drily. Some people in the room were scandalized by this sexy reference, but Minnie thought she understood perfectly well what her daughter-in-law felt. The two women had not yet crystallized their relationship. In some ways, they saw eye to eye. Yet in others . . . Each had a strong personality and each usually formed strong opinions about other people. But they were still sizing each other up.

Ray sat, tipping back the front legs of a wooden chair and swapping travel anecdotes with Arturo, a Sicilian who had worked in construction gangs in Africa and South America before settling in the United States. Ray's travel experience was more limited. He had toured Europe and North Africa, lived in Italy for six months, and spent a short time working among American Indians in the Southwest. He made the trip to Europe during his convalescence from the serious injuries he had suffered three years before at the hands of his father's murderer—a man who had also been bent on killing him. It was an episode the family preferred to forget.

He met Cynthia on the plane trip back to the States. She was an American Airlines stewardess on the Rome–New York run. A new-wave stewardess. She spilled coffee in his lap and then had the nerve to blame him for having stuck his foot into the aisle. They had dinner together at Benito's the very next evening. He learned that she had been a French literature and language major, that she hated her airlines job, had a passion for gothic novels and potato chips, and had published poetry in an obscure literary magazine. The coffee-spilling incident set the tone of their relationship. It was based on lively disagreement.

Anthony Mancini

During the dinner date, they argued about the relative merits of French and Italian culture. It was Proust versus Pincherle, Dior versus Valentino, Mallarme against Montale. She brought up French haute cuisine. He countered with Florentine recipes and Abruzzese chefs. He had her boiling like a neglected tea kettle by the time he had finished giving her his views that the two greatest Frenchmen in history were Bonaparte and Mazarin, both Italians, that Paris was a small fishing village when the Roman legions first marched into the city, and that the great modern Paris was designed by a German.

By some miracle, they wound up in her apartment. In bed.

It was a typhoon courtship—disputation and sex. To settle things, they got married.

Ray, who had the instincts of a reformer, got a job as a trial lawyer with the Legal Aid Society. Cynthia gave up her airlines job to work as a UN guide, writing poetry in her spare time. She was angling for an interpreter's post in the Security Council when she got pregnant. There were budget cuts at Legal Aid, so Ray was out of a job. They went to Baton Rouge, where the baby was born.

Now they had returned to Little Italy, where Ray was to "put down roots." He bought a loft on Broome Street that he planned to renovate bit by bit, while he and his family camped out at Minnie's place. He was going to put out his shingle in the neighborhood, become an old-style neighborhood lawyer with new-style social ideals.

Cynthia was dubious. She wondered about the practicality of raising a child in a neighborhood with few parks and nursery schools. Ray argued that a lot of children lived in Little Italy, as well as in neighboring SoHo and Greenwich Village. Then he would break out his litany of neighborhood merits—the fine restaurants, both Italian and Chinese, the convenient transportation, the specialty food shops, etcetera. "Not to mention its providing the kid the chance of growing up with a sense of himself, of his origins.."

"I know, I know," Cynthia would respond. "Ethnic identi-

Minnie Santangelo and the Evil Eye

ty. Roots. He'll be a seasoned veteran of the mean streets. Why don't we get him one of those tricolor buttons that say, 'I'm proud to be Italian.' We'll pin it to his bib."

"Why not?" said Ray.

She put on a mock thoughtful face, touching her chin with her forefinger. "Do you think they make buttons saying, 'I'm proud to be half-Italian'?"

In the end they did it his way. Partly because she secretly thought there might be something to what he said, but also because there was still much of the pliant southern belle in her. More than she was comfortable with.

And Stefano seemed to thrive in the environment. The baby was giggling now, dandled on the copious knees of Angela Treponti, Ray's widowed aunt. She was a woman with the personality of a rich pastry and a figure to match. She was singing the child an Italian nursery rhyme, *Bello chi dorme al letto di fiori.* Beautiful is he who sleeps on a bed of flowers. "And this kid would be beautiful in a garbage dump, I tell you," Aunt Angela said in her most operatic manner. "Never in my life have I seen such a handsome baby. Eyes like sterling silver. And what a face. An angel. A cherub by Raffaello."

"*Zia,*" said Ray with a laugh to mask his pride. "Don't forget his peachblow complexion, his Da Vinci proportions."

She paid him no mind. "Intelligent, too." She positioned the baby on her knees to look into his eyes. "See how he looks at me when I talk, notices everything. I predict he will be brilliant. I predict it."

Minnie had come in from the kitchen bearing a platter of spaghetti with wisps of smoke rising from it. "Who's the grandma here, anyhow, Angela? Me or you?"

"You're the lucky one," Angela said with a look of sad resignation. She brightened. "But I am to be his *comare.* A godmother has certain rights and privileges, you know. He is the image of my brother. The image of his grandfather."

Angela was Minnie's late husband's half-sister by his mother's first marriage, and a frequent visitor to the Santangelo household over the years. In answer to Minnie's dinner call, she was now trying to hoist her bulk up from an upholstered chair. Little Stefano had been passed along to Sister Anastasia, who cradled the baby gingerly in one arm as she held on to her glass of Campari.

Despite the relaxation of dress codes for nuns, Sister Anastasia still wore wimple and habit. But she did so more out of inertia than from any resistance to change. She was in fact oblivious to such things. There were often, as now, food stains on her faded white wimple, and wisps of gray hair stuck out from under the headdress.

The nun was sharp-featured and thin as a cornstalk. The black habit enhanced her cronelike appearance. She was also the immigration sponsor of and surrogate mother to Fortunato Ricci, known in the neighborhood as *Il Gobbo*—the dwarf.

Minnie asked Sister Anastasia, "Where is Fortunato today? I wish he could have come to see the baby."

The nun handed Stefano over to his mother who unceremoniously plunked him down in a high chair and tied a bib around his neck.

"You know him," the nun said, peering into her glass. "He doesn't like these gatherings. I think he's in Corallo's café, reading magazines."

"That's no way to spend a Sunday," said Minnie, serving steaming portions of pasta to the guests who sat down at a dining table she had placed in a corner of the living room. They usually ate in the kitchen except for special occasions. Doctor Bevilaqua, a graduate of the University of Bologna medical school, could not resist a small dissertation on the therapeutic value of pasta. "Spaghetti like this," he said in a melodic falsetto, "made at home with love, is better than all the miracle drugs of today." With exaggerated signs of pleasure, he sniffed the portion Minnie was heaping on his plate and tucked a cloth napkin into his shirt collar. "You are an artist and a scientist, Signora. Of the first order."

Minnie Santangelo and the Evil Eye

Flushed with pride and with her labors, Minnie set a plate of spaghetti before her grandson. "You keep up your flattery, *Dottore*, and you'll have to treat me for a badly swelled head."

Bevilaqua twirled his fork. "I'll ask a reasonable fee—two plates for a house call, one for an office visit."

"Save room for the meat," Minnie admonished everyone.

And so they began to eat.

Chapter 4

The white linen tablecloth was littered with the casualties of the meal—blotches of red sauce, limp celery stalks, mutilated fruit. The odor of garlic had been supplanted by the mightier scent of anise from the sambucca liqueur and loud festivity gave way to droning satiety.

Most of the guests had gone. Ray and Cynthia were off on a stroll to Grennwich Village while Arturo, Angela, and Minnie lingered over a third cup of coffee.

"Minootch," sighed Arturo after a long silence. "It was a good meal and a good time."

"We'll have an even better time next week at the christening," Minnie promised, gazing down at the baby who was asleep by the open window. He lay in an old-fashioned wooden crib that his parents had bought in an antique shop down South. His eyelids fluttered in sleep.

"You bet your life," agreed Arturo, using one of his pet English phrases. The corners of his small brown eyes crinkled as he smiled. "I'm gonna buy me a new suit."

Minnie pouted. "Don't spend money needlessly, Artur'."

Anthony Mancini

"No sir," he insisted. "This is an important day for me, too. I've never been a *compare* before." He struck the Italian word for "godfather" like a cymbal.

Minnie smiled affectionately. Arturo was an old friend with no family of his own who had sort of adopted Minnie and Ray, and his pride in Stefano equaled that of any grandfather. She knew he would take the godfather role seriously, which had prompted her in the first place to ask Ray to choose him. Ray needed no coaxing for he and Arturo had been very close, especially since Ray's father's death.

Arturo was overjoyed. He had a keen appreciation of the honor involved. To southern Italians, a people for whom God and country take a back seat to kinship, *comparaggio* has great significance. The connection almost transcends consanguinity. To become a freely chosen brother or sister, a surrogate parent, is a request nearly impossible to deny. *Comparaggio* is a fellowship against a pitiless nature, alien oppression, and intangible evil forces. When worse came to worst, Arturo knew Stefano would turn to his godfather or godmother.

Arturo was an ideal candidate for the role. He had a beardless face and inscrutable eyes like an old Indian shaman, and a zookeeper's power over birds and animals. In his small apartment he kept two cats, a slant-eyed mongrel who looked part wolf, and a cockatoo. In the outward observances of the faith he was religious as few men of the community were. But, like his Sicilian ancestors, he mingled Christianity in the spiritual caldron with older beliefs.

His smile dissolved into a look of seriousness. He fished in his jacket pocket, producing a small box. "Something for the child."

"But the gifts don't come till the baptism," protested Aunt Angela, the future godmother, who had been sitting quietly and knitting, her usual pastime when she was not eating.

"This is not a baptism gift," he explained. "This is something very different." He opened the box and drew out an object, dangling it by a gold chain. It was a coral horn, small and bright red.

"*Un corno,*" said Minnie.

"Right," said Arturo. "We could put it on now, while he's still asleep."

Angela frowned. "*Sciochezza,*" she said. "Such silliness. These are modern times, you know." She shook her head in disapproval over her deft needlework.

"Do you mean it seriously?" Minnie asked. "Against the *malocchio?*"

He looked up from the dangling horn into Minnie's eyes. "Sure, it's serious. We don't want anything to happen to the baby. Let's play it safe."

Suspicion narrowed Minnie's eyes. "Why didn't you give it to him while the mother was here?"

He looked a little sheepish. "She might not understand such things. You can explain it to her better than I."

"A nice religious medal would have been much better," Angela observed ill-temperedly, as the needles flurried. "That's what *I* will get him."

Arturo parried her frown with one of his own. "Why can't he have both?"

"Thou shalt not take strange gods before me," Angela said pompously.

"Now the Vatican says that Saint Christopher is a 'strange god'," he pointed out, "but you still have a Saint Christopher medal hanging over the dashboard of your car."

Angela began a riposte, then settled for drawing her penciled eyebrows together.

Minnie saw no harm in the amulet; one *always* heard stories of the unexplained. She remembered as a little girl in her native village the tale of the *strega*, the witch, in the nearby town and about the child who took ill. She fancied herself too modern to fully believe the stories, but Arturo's feelings might be hurt.

"You put it on him, Artur'," Minnie said.

"Be careful not to wake the child," Angela admonished.

Arturo walked with a serious air over to the crib and slipped the chain carefully around the sleeping child's neck. He fastened the clasp. The baby didn't stir. *"Se malocchio non ci fosse,"* he pronounced "To ward off the evil eye."

"Sciochezza," said Angela, under her breath. "Nonsense."

"More coffee?" asked Minnie without enthusiasm since it was getting late.

"Not for me," said Angela, bundling up her knitting and cramming it into the tote bag at her feet. "I need my beauty sleep."

"Will you give an old superstitious man a lift home?" Arturo asked.

"Why not?" Angela cracked a smile. Then it disappeared as her eyes fastened on a corner of the kitchen near the refrigerator.

"What's the matter?" Minnie asked.

Without replying, she calmly put down her bag, grabbed a broom leaning against the counter, and stealthily walked over to the refrigerator as Minnie and Arturo watched dumbfounded. The broom handle flashed.

A look of satisfaction passed Angela's face as she serenely put down the broom and picked up her tote bag. "Let's go, Arturo."

In the corner lay a dead rat.

Chapter 5

As usual on Monday night, the basement of Saint Theresa's sounded like a bird sanctuary, as the neighborhood women flocked to the weekly bingo game. They chattered in a babble of English, Italian, Sicilian, and Neapolitan over the screech of bridge chairs being pulled up to the long folding tables. They traded news of ailments, operations, trips, births, deaths, bargains, and scandals with as much efficiency as a community newspaper.

Minnie, Angela, and Arturo had set their bingo cards down before them. They had already commented on a neighborhood girl runaway, a childbirth after only seven months of marriage, Angela's varicose veins, the price of veal, and the latest development in a favorite soap opera. Arturo, one of the few men who regularly attended bingo night, contributed a running philosophical commentary.

Carmela Paoli twirled the drum and called the first number: "G-fifty-one."

"OOh, I gotta G-fifty-one," crowed Angela. "Invite everybody to the baptism yet, Minnie?"

"I always start off bad," Minnie sighed. "Never get the first number. *Sure* I invited everybody. It's gonna be a big day."

"A lot of people, huh?" Arturo said, fiddling with his markers.

"Everyone will be there," said Minnie. "From Father Mancuso to Fortunato."

"Fortunato Ricci?" Angela asked.

"Yes. Of course."

"He gives me the creeps," Angela said.

"Why?" Minnie protested. "He's a good soul. Just because he's . . . "

"B-seventy," announced Carmela.

"This is my lucky night," said Angela, putting another marker down. "It's not that, Minnie. *He*'s so unpleasant."

"Not when you get to know him."

Arturo looked somber. "Do you really think it's a good idea? You know what they say about him."

Minnie looked up from her bingo board. "No. What do they say?"

"He's a *jettatore.*"

"*Stupidaggine,*" said Minnie. "Such nonsense."

Arturo shrugged sagaciously. "You never know about these things. Even he himself says so."

"He likes me," Minnie insisted. "He wouldn't do anything to hurt me or my family. He's very gentle, really. This is just prejudice because of his physical problem."

"Maybe you're right. But, according to the old ways, he doesn't have to wish you evil to cast the evil eye. He may be an involuntary thrower. A *jettatore* despite himself—not evil himself, but cursed with the power of *il Fascino*. The fascination."

"N-sixty."

"I got that number," said Arturo.

Minnie's mouth curved downward. "I don't believe it. He's a good man. I won't say that it's all superstition, these beliefs.

But you can't convince me that evil can come from a good man."

"He would ruin the party, *malocchio* or no," said Angela. "Or at least bring bad luck."

"Evil can come from good," said Arturo solemnly. "It's sometimes the way of life. You are too naive, Minerva."

"I always thought the evil eye was thrown by women," said Minnie.

"Mostly but not always," he said. "In tradition, it is sometimes a dwarf. It is usually someone who was born with the power—or the affliction, however you view it. And it is usually someone who has good reason to be jealous of other people."

"B-thirty-six," announced Carmela. This time Minnie had the number. With a distracted air, she placed the marker down. She felt guilty at doubting her instincts about Fortunato. People like him encountered enough prejudice in their lives. She wondered if she wasn't patronizing him. Here the dwarf was linked to supernatural evil merely because of his deformity. Her better nature rebelled against the notion, but she found one side of herself believing, and it disturbed her.

"I won't discuss it," Minnie said. "Fortunato is welcome to the party, just like all my other friends."

Arturo shurgged. "Maybe he won't come."

"Maybe he won't," said Minnie. "But he's welcome all the same. And I'm going to urge him to make it."

"It's the baby's welfare I'm considering," said Arturo.

Minnie felt a twinge of fear. "The baby will do just fine. Everybody will have a good time."

"Well, I won't," Angela protested, "if Fortunato Ricci comes. This *malocchio* stuff is foolishness. But that man is not the type for a party. He's a sourpuss."

"I-forty-two," said Carmela.

"He's coming," Minnie said with all the conviction she could muster. "He's coming and I won't hear another word."

"O-eighty-two" was the next number.

"Bingo," said an excited voice two tables down. The woman in the slouch hat who went up to collect the prize—a blender—acted like she was getting an Academy Award.

Arturo's finely tuned instincts told him something important was going to happen at the christening, but he didn't know how to make Minnie believe him. He felt no animosity toward Fortunato, but he had along with his other talents the gift of premonition. He was still close to the peasant world of his origins, where harsh circumstances begot mysticism—where in the face of drought, political oppression, malaria, and social exploitation, there was refuge in passivity, acceptance of the inevitable, and an understanding of the uses of magic. In the war against Nature, the peasants of southern Italy surrendered to her and found comfort in her coils. Some became one with the wolf and the wild goat. Arturo was one of them.

He smiled at Minnie, whose face betrayed concern. Under his smile, the frown dissolved and she allowed herself a smile too.

"Fortunato may be harmless ," he said reassuringly.

Minnie nodded. But she felt uneasy, as she had on the day before the homecoming. Minnie had the talent too.

Chapter 6

Remo Santangelo was a man who reveled in the drama of life, not in its intermissions. So he was destined to be an activist. There are some who enter politics and public life to relive and avenge an old grievance, or right an old wrong. Ray was in it because it was a cockfight.

Not that he hadn't strongly held convictions and compassion for his kind. He did, all right. In fact, he wore his chauvinism brashly, like a flower in his buttonhole. But chauvinism was still mainly the actor's costume, the cock's preening feather. It was the teeth that won the fight. Ray had teeth.

He was named after one of the twins who founded Rome. His brother Romolo died in childbirth to Minnie, that good she-wolf who suckled Ray alone. So he felt he had to live intensely enough for two, if only to justify the double dose of love he got.

Ray was being introspective now, a rare event—perhaps because he was walking by the ocean. Risking pompousness, he allowed himself to reflect that the sea makes philosophers of us all. But how could he be a philosopher with the sights before him—white string bikinis testing the surf, slim ankles drawn up sharply in coy pain as vulnerable flesh met cold water—supple thighs, nubile breasts.

"Lust," he screamed into the surf.

"What?" said his understanding wife, pretending not to understand.

"You heard what I said," he growled, turning to her with a stage leer. He crossed his eyes and stuck out his tongue. They continued to walk by the water's edge. He was carrying a collapsible playpen, air mattress, three towels, and an umbrella. She followed a few steps behind, carrying the baby and two beach chairs. Minnie, wearing a modest one-piece skirted bathing suit with green flowers on it and a wide straw hat, brought up the rear. She carried an army blanket, cooler, and picnic basket. Despite her freight and the merciless sun, she walked with straight posture and regular breath. A breeze skimmed the ocean and whipped back her wavy hair. The swirl of surf lapped at her feet and was tugged back by the insistent tide.

"This spot looks okay," Ray said, dropping his burden and stretching indolently. He peered at his family through tinted aviator glasses. "All right with you?"

"Sure," said Minnie, unburdening.

Cynthia surveyed the area. "I guess this is okay. I like to be a little farther from the water."

"Sorry we have no bayous and deltas here," Ray said.

She handed the baby to Minnie and dropped her red oriental robe on the beach chair. She wore a pea-green bikini and a gold band around her long neck. She dug her heels into the sand and stretched. She had a long-limbed, fibrous body. The cords by which muscles were attached to bones appeared and rippled at the slightest movement. She produced an Afro comb and began teasing her tight red curls. Sinews scurried like live insects over her brown body.

"This is a nice beach," Minnie said. "Not too many people."

They had come to the far end of Jones Beach near the Robert Moses causeway, after parking the car illegally among the dunes and shrubbery.

The day was crystal, a lambent thing. A fresh breeze came from the south. Ray, whistling and in high spirits, ground the umbrella into the sand while Cynthia set up the playpen in its shade. She took the baby from Minnie's arms and stripped off every stitch of the child's clothes. Stefano yawned and stretched in a remarkably grown-up way. The he burst into a smile.

Ray shook his head in amazement. "Don't you ever cry or anything, you bugger you?"

Cynthia had her hands on her hips, looking down at the child with a smile. "He likes the beach."

"A regular beach bum," Ray said.

The baby had been sitting with the shaky equilibrium of a six-month-old. Still smiling, he toppled onto his right side, getting sand on his cheek and in between the folds of flesh on his neck. Cynthia bent over the playpen and began to wipe the sand off with a towel. She noticed the amulet. Minnie had fed and washed him that morning.

Cynthia looked suspicously at her mother-in-law. "What's that thing around his neck?"

Minnie reddened slightly. "Just a little trinket. A gift from Arturo. I forgot to tell you about it."

Cynthia fingered the ornament. "It's ugly." She frowned. "I hate to hurt the old guy's feelings."

Ray was curious. "Let me have a look." He held the amulet between his thumb and forefinger. "Isn't this a talisman of some sort? Against *malocchio?*"

Cynthia's bold eyebrows came together. "What's *malocchio?*"

Ray looked at his wife. "The evil eye."

"Not seriously?" she asked cynically.
"In a way it's serious," he said. "It's traditional."
"Ridiculous," she said.
"It's harmless. Don't be so intolerant."
"He might get a rash from it," she said, pursing her lips.

Minnie was unpacking the picnic lunch. "Who wants a sandwich? Capicola. It's fresh. A nice chicken leg?"

"You're overprotective," Ray said to Cynthia.

"*Me* overprotective?" she replied, her voice climbing to a higher register. "How about this voodoo charm?"

"Don't patronize. It looks cute on the kid."

"I think it should come off," Cynthia said.

"Anybody want a plum?" Minnie offered.

"It's too early to eat," said Ray. "Let's keep it on him. Think of Arturo."

Cynthia's face softened. She liked Arturo and it wasn't worth having a big fight about. "Maybe for a while."

"At least until the baptism," Ray said. "He's the *compare*, after all."

"I suppose it will do no harm. Although I don't like to encourage such things." She turned to Minnie. "I didn't realize that Arturo was . . . well, so superstitious." She lay down on the blanket and faced the sun. "He seems so sensible. And sweet."

Minnie bit into a chicken leg. "He is sensible and sweet."

"Rub some Sea and Ski on my back, will you, Ray?" said Cynthia. "Does the horn have symbolic value? Sentimental value?"

With an air of distraction, Minnie brushed sand from her thigh. "You could say so. But it's really more than that."

Cynthia propped herself up on her elbows as Ray applied the lotion. "You don't mean he actually *believes* in the evil eye."

"It's hard to answer you," Minnie said hesitantly. She groped for the right words under the ardent rays of the sun. "Arturo may seem simple to you. But he has seen many things in his life that are not entirely explained by conventional science. To him, not all explanations are material, you know?"

"Metaphysics, okay," said Cynthia. "But what *is* he? Some kind of medicine man?"

"To use one kind of medicine does not rule out another," Minnie said. "It's good to play it safe."

"Propitiate all the gods," said Ray.

Minnie jabbed her thumb in his direction. "He talks better than me."

"Any beer in that cooler?" he asked, wiping excess suntan lotion from his fingers with a paper napkin. Minnie handed him a can of beer. *Pop and fizz.*

Cynthia squinted into the sun. Freckles were beginning to sprout on her nose. "I'm a Catholic," she said. "I was taught there's only one God."

"Sure," Ray drawled. "And three persons in that one God, a goddess named Mary, an army of saints and angels. Gets crowded up there in your monotheistic heaven." Her smile conceded the point. "Let's see," he continued "the doctrine of transubstantiation . . . Bread and wine turn into the body and blood of Christ. That's not superstition, that's a mystery. And holy water, that's not like garlic against evil. Religious medals are nothing like amulets."

"Okay, you made your point," Cynthia said.

Minnie frowned at him. "Don't blaspheme."

"I'm not knocking it, Mamma," he assured her. "Just making a point." He sprang to his feet. "Let's go into the water, Cynthia."

She uncoiled her long legs. "Last one in's a Sardinian medicine man."

Minnie watched the backs of their heels kicking up sand. Slim bodies knifed the water. Minnie looked at her grandson who made a contented humming noise as he played with a keychain. She tugged at a tendon in the chicken leg with her small front teeth and reflected under the punishing sun.

Chapter 7

The women sat brooding, hens in the hatchery. The girl's hour drew near. The husband's mother and grandmother had also come from the village over the hill to be there when she delivered. In the room adjoining the girl's bedroom, they sat on straight chairs and looked out a window streaked with fly tracks at the craggy landscape of Campania. They drank camomile with looks of mistrust on their wrinkled faces. The girl's brother, that battered bird of a boy, stood by the door to the bedroom with the usual frightened look on his face. Only the mother was allowed in the delivery room with the doctor.

Eva the serving girl had gone to the fountain in the village square for water. She was wrapped in a black shawl against the whipping wind. She brought back the water jug balanced on her head. The sun was a ball of flame on the flat western horizon. The villagers of Montevecchio, refreshed by afternoon naps, gathered in the square for coffee, tobacco, and gossip. They all watched Eva's straightly held body as she walked back to the house. They didn't care if misfortune came to this house of gentry, but they were careful to avoid malediction. In these parts, they had known for centuries that expressed evil wishes could boomerang.

Eva knew what they were thinking. She too was a peasant, though loyal to the landowning family. She was the illegitimate child of a *contadina* who had died when Eva was only two, and she had lived in the grand stone house ever since. She was four years old. As she ascended the small flight of steps leading to the front door, she was acutely aware of the eyes upon her. Being the focus of village interest filled her with a strange sense of pride. Her supple body swayed to the music of recognition.

The wooden door led to a shuttered living room with lower ceilings than the outside of the building suggested. Tile covered the floors, and the walls and ceilings were of white stone, lending the house a Moorish flavor. Gilt sconces jutted from the rough stone wall. She climbed a wrought-iron staircase to the bedroom, passing faded oil paintings of ancestors. Their patina of age came from nature's benevolent brush—garish pictures of one era transformed into the mellow portraits of another. She knocked on the door of the delivery room.

It opened to the vast form of Dottore Parini, who waved her in with a sweep of the arm. The doctor was an implacable irredentist and a self-important man. Puff and swagger was his style.

Eva wondered what all the fuss was about. Birth was like death, neither to be welcomed nor shunned. On reflection, though, she too felt an inner excitement. There was something different about this delivery.

The girl on the bed shone with sweat. Her body was still but rigid. She was about to start the final contractions. Eva placed the jar of water on the tile floor near the bed. The doctor instructed her to sit in a chair by the wall until he called her. She had been chosen to assist in the birth. Parini's presence here was unusual in any case, for in most births even landowners called in a midwife. That was one of the things the villagers resented about this family. They often broke custom for the sake of appearances. In Montevecchio, it was not advisable to try to seem better than others.

With elaborate flourish, Dottore Parini went about his work. Eva made certain her indifference let him know that she was not impressed. She was scornful. The people of this area stood in awe neither of priest nor doctor. Other professions— for lack of a better word—had already cornered the market on their respect.

Eventually even the mother was sent out of the room. She left in a huff but not out of concern for her daughter. Her sense of rank had been offended. When she joined the others in the anteroom, they didn't even raise their eyebrows. The in-laws sipped tea in silence, secretly hoping the hostess would commit a breach of protocol. Inwardly, they were rehearsing complaints to the soldier son, the father of the child. He was on the Ethiopian front.

Eva watched expectantly as the doctor instructed the girl on how to breathe. The contractions were coming more and more rapidly now, and Parini beckoned to Eva. Forceps lay gleaming on the bedside table. Eva was fearful as she edged toward the bed. She had assisted in many other childbirths in her sixteen years. But somehow this was different. The pregnant girl's breathing became strained and she bit her upper lip. The shadow of the doctor's great bulk fell over her writhing body.

"Now push," he ordered. "Push."

In the anteroom, the mother looked thoughtfully out the window to hills haloed by the setting sun. She would have a grandson. She knew she would have a grandson. But fear, a hungry mouse, gnawed at her. Had the healer come in time those months before when her daughter had fallen ill? Life in this place was full of peril. The State took its taxes and conscripted the men. And the barren soil took its toll of the spirit. But there were even more insidious dangers astalk here. Ill will and malediction ranged the countryside. Her daughter's groans reached her ears and she heard the snuffling of pigs in the barn outside. The mother prayed to the Christian God and the woodland spirits as well that the healer's power had been stronger than the other forces at work.

Suddenly she knew that it was over. No sound came from the delivery room. A stillness, a finality, hung in the air. They waited another fifteen minutes before the doctor came out. The mother rose from her chair while the in-laws kept their seats, shifting their buttocks forward to the edge of the chairs.

The doctor's eyes burned under his bushy brows. The mother's heart sank. *"Signore,"* he said, addressing all the women. "A word with you in another room."

Eva had not been quite sure what was wrong, but she knew it was serious. The serving girl neither mourned nor felt satisfaction over it. She had dreamed of a goat last night and this outcome was inevitable. As figs dry in the sun and the carcass of a dead cow rots, so must this process evolve. Inevitable. She thought of the soldier husband. The sourness of his breath, his thin, snakelike penis. She should have had his child. Eva looked down at the girl, now sleeping calmly. She had come out of it fine. For now. With no sign of emotion, Eva spat on the floor. Then she gathered up her skirts and left the room.

The mother maintained a resigned façade. No tears. Her mouth was an impassive line, her body rigidly under control. Only the pupils of her speckled brown eyes, glowing with grievance, betrayed her feelings.

Dottore Parini was not the sort to dispense consolation. He spoke no words of sympathy but went about his business with an air of disinterest. He stayed for an hour until the girl had awakened and was ready to nurse her child. The baby, wrapped in a blanket, was in Eva's arms. She and the doctor went into the girl's room.

The others sat outside again, waiting, knowing. The husband's relatives shot hot glances at each other, flashing a shared revulsion of this accursed family. A minute later, the girl's bestial scream rang through the gathering night.

Chapter 8

Italian-American neighborhoods are much like the gnarled old peasants who settled there. They seem to live on longer than most. And Little Italy is the most venerable of them all. Of course, there are many churches in the archetypal transplanted village. Saint Theresa's, where Stefano Santangelo was to be baptized this tinfoil summer morning, is one of them.

It was not quiet in church. With relatives and neighbors congregating, a lusty greeting often rang out amid the murmurs. It seemed more that a party was beginning than a religious service. But a hush descended when the guest of honor arrived.

He was borne in the arms of Arturo Longo as Angela Treponti hovered nearby. With an air of happy solemnity, they scaled the steps of Saint Theresa's and were greeted at the front door by Father Mancuso, who beamed with pleasure. It was the guest's first visit.

The godparents muttered a standard prayer, asking faith from God in the name of the child. The priest breathed upon the baby's face, an exorcism for the innocent. On the infant's forehead and breast he made the sign of the cross with his fingers, redeeming him who has not yet been lost. After the imposition of hands, an act he performed with proper sacerdotal flourish, Father Mancuso placed a pinch of blessed salt on the child's mouth. It was meant to make him relish good works. The priest then put his violet stole over the child and ushered them all indoors.

Down a side aisle of the church, the godparents prayed together, professing faith for the wordless baby. The priest now touched the ears and nostrils of little Stefano with spittle in place of biblical clay. Then he led the child to the baptismal font to be washed vicariously in the waters of Siloe.

Behind a side altar rail the font sat like a big cup on a stone pedestal that bore a bas relief depicting John the Baptist holding a hooked staff and pouring water over the head of Christ. Father Mancuso asked the godparents to speak for the child and "renounce Satan, his works and his pomps." Three times they pledged this. The priest anointed the child on the breast with the oil of the cathecumens, a mixture of olive oil and chrism—an oil based in balsam. The godparents now declared faith for Stefano and asked for baptism. Having changed his violet stole for a white one, Father Mancuso took water from the font, made the sign of the cross three times, and laved the child's forehead.

Over the sound of the baby's wailing, Father Mancuso said, "I baptize thee Stefano Arturo in the name of the Father and of the Son and of the Holy Ghost." Arturo, in a new tan double-knit suit, cradled the baby gingerly. His eyes glowed like candles. Angela's hand held the baby's curled fist. She wore peach-colored chiffon and a serious expression.

A thrill ran through Minnie, standing in the first circle of onlookers. She clutched a lace handkerchief and forced a smile through her emotion. A nervous hand fluffed her permanent-waved hair. Remo grinned casually. His left arm gripped his mother's shoulder and his right rested on his wife's waist. Cynthia performed her usual balancing act of moods, looking both alert and mildly bored. Her face was friendly. She was not pretty, but she had a touch of beauty and she knew the value of a smile.

The congregation murmured their approval. One young woman stood quietly five pews down from the font. Nobody seemed to notice her staring intently at the child. Her eyes were molten metal. Her eyes.

The baby howled.

Minnie flinched.

The priest anointed the crown of the child's head with chrism. Then he placed a white veil on Stefano's head with the words, "Receive this white garment which mayest thou carry without stain before the judgment seat of Our Lord Jesus Christ, that thou mayest have eternal life. Amen."

The young woman's eyes burned.

"Go in peace," the priest said to the wailing child.

Minnie trembled. She realized it was the first time she had ever heard her grandson cry.

Chapter 9

In her kitchen today, Minnie was *maestra*. She would see to it that this meal would be a *panarda*, a bout of eating worthy of her untamed mountain homeland of Abruzzi. On the day when Stefano officially became a Christian, they would celebrate as in the old days, with a heathen orgy of food.

"*Favorisca,*" Minnie said, welcoming a guest with careful formality. "So happy you came."

It was Father Mancuso who had entered the kitchen to pay respects to his hostess—and to savor the food. Like Doctor Bevilaqua, the priest was an epicure and therefore devoted to Minnie. When his usually morose face lit up in a smile, it was like a crescent moon appearing from behind a cloud.

His eyes swept over the cornucopious scene. "Ah, Signora," he said, eyes darting from pasta to pies, "what a picture this makes." Gingerly, he picked up a wooden spoon and dipped it into the bubbling tomato sauce. He tasted it with a sucking sound, for it was very hot. "Perfection," he judged.

Minnie laughed. "Anyone can see that you are *Abruzzese.*"

Diffidently, he scratched his balding pate. "It is apparent. Above all, we are famous for the digestive tract."

The sink was already cluttered with pots and pans. All four burners on the old gas stove were ablaze. The round wooden table in the middle of the room, where Minnie took most of her solitary meals, was stacked with a Medusa's head of homemade *maccheroni* noodles. To the side of the pile lay the *chitarra*, the lyrelike instrument on which she cut the pasta. A vase of sweet red peppers, a pepper grinder, and three ripe tomatoes shared the space.

The sideboard where the statue of Saint Anthony stood was covered with prepared dishes. There was a potato and cheese pie, the *timballo di scamorza*, a plate of stuffed veal with white beans, a *timballo di melanzane* or eggplant, ham and cheese, a pan of deep-fried potatoes, fried jam cushion Teramo style, and a *parozzo*, an almond and chocolate layer cake, a dessert praised by the poet D'Annunzio. Saint Anthony's nose was smudged with flour.

Near the window overlooking the street was a borrowed charcoal rotisserie turning the main course of this merciless meal: a *porchetta*—a huge roast suckling pig, complete with apple in its mournful mouth. The crisp brown color of its sad eye sockets and the soft texture of the meat where the forelegs had been amputated showed it was almost done.

Minnie checked the tomato sauce and sniffed the celery soup. Mancuso cradled a bottle of wine in his forearm. "Montepulciano," he said admiringly. "I haven't seen a bottle of this stuff since the old country. Where in heaven did you get it?"

"Not in heaven." Minnie was clearly delighted. "Remo ordered it through an uptown place. A fancy wine shop."

"And, *Dio mio*," he said, catching sight of the rounded, narrow-necked bottle of green liqueur. "Centerbe, the drink of a hundred herbs. Did Remo get this too?"

Minnie shook her head. "I saved that from my husband's

stock." Extending her pudgy arm, she gestured at the opulence around her. "It will help us digest all this."

"It is potent stuff. This dinner is an authentic *panarda*, eh? I feel like a sinful pagan."

Sounds of laughter and talking came from the living room where other guests were assembling. The furniture had been pushed aside to make room for two long bridge tables covered with off-white damask. The napkins were cloth and the cutlery silver. The crystal glasses had been taken down from the top shelf of the cupboard and polished individually until they winked.

The guests were already primed. Dr. Bevilaqua was chomping celery and pinching Cynthia's behind. In vain, Arturo had been trying to get Sister Anastasia to dance a fox-trot. "Find a more experienced partner," the nun advised him, returning to nurse her dry thoughts and sweet vermouth. Arturo frowned sadly.

Ray had one eye on the New York Yankees beating the Big Red machine and another on Bevilaqua. He tried to be flattered. And baby Stefano was ensconced on a sofa, like a prince at a beggars' banquet.

He sat, a cherub in a cloud of pillows. Dangling from the ceiling was a mobile of plastic butterflies that he set in motion with a swipe of the hand. He had on old-fashioned clothes, a white gown with lace tatting. His soon-to-be gray eyes looked out on the world with a new ability to see things distinctly. Fingers of benevolent giants chucked him under the chin. Great faces loomed above him, nostrils dilating, mouths moving, producing soft sounds. Lips were pressed against his satin cheek. A swirl of sounds, smells, colors, forms in the new world.

Ray had distracted Bevilaqua from his wife's ass by contriving to resume an earlier conversation. "You must look closely," the doctor said, "at the Aristotelian message of Gertrude Stein: 'a rose is a rose is a rose.' "

Ray frowned. "It won't come easily. I'm a born Platonist."

And so they wandered in the world of amateur philosophy until all conversation was interrupted by the theatrical entrance of Aunt Angela. She had arrived late with a waterfall of apologies and a gift of peacock feathers that she arranged in a vase and placed on an end table. Then she made straight for Stefano.

"Oh, he's so beautiful," Aunt Angela said, stroking the baby's cheek. "He will do great things, mark my words. You are so lucky, Minerva." She peered at the child. "He will have gray eyes."

Angela settled her big body in a canvas chair. Satisfaction shone on her face. She had gotten fat over the years but her pretty features had survived the siege of time. She had long lashes and a small, symmetrical nose. "A widow like me," she sighed, "needs someone to dote on."

"You're a godmother now," Minnie said, "you can call yourself that instead of a widow."

Angela beamed. "I like it better, too."

"Have a drink of something," urged Minnie. "We already started celebrating."

"Mustn't fall behind," said Angela, and she accepted a glass of vermouth. "*Salute.* To Stefano." She drank it down.

Doctor Bevilaqua rubbed his hands together. "When do we eat?" he asked, throwing caution—and all thought of his gout—to the wind.

"Soon," said Minnie. "All the guests haven't arrived."

"Who's missing?" Arturo asked.

"Fortunato," she said, turning to the nun who was looking blankly into a glass. "It's late. Isn't he coming?"

Sister Anastasia shrugged, somehow making the gesture a mixture of defiance and defensiveness. "Maybe, maybe not. He doesn't make decisions until the last minute. And he never tells me what they are."

Minnie Santangelo and the Evil Eye

"He'll be here soon," said Minnie, puttering around the table. "Let's wait."

Arturo's eyes followed her—eyes like trapdoors to a sunless place. Angela made a sour face at the prospect of Fortunato. Sister Anastasia fixed her eyes on the bottom of her glass while Ray and the priest discussed ecclesiastical law and Doctor Bevilaqua grabbed an anchovy from the antipasto.

They waited until the hunchback knocked on the door.

Minnie greeted him effusively, but his response was a cryptic nod. He wore a tie and a suit jacket over his sickle-shaped body, and his mouth was set in a dignified line. He carried a white cardboard box of pastry.

"*Benvenuto*," said Minnie. "Welcome. You are just in time. It's too hot for a jacket. Hang it on that hook there, and make yourself at home." She turned to the other guests. "Fortunato is here."

They murmured greetings.

Ray came over and extended his hand. "My old poker opponent. How are things?"

Fortunato limply touched Ray's hand. "Welcome home."

Ray nodded in Cynthia's direction. "My wife, Cynthia. Cynthia, I want you to meet Fortunato."

She smiled perfunctorily and nodded, without rising from the couch. Her stemlike legs were crossed. Fortunato, with a gallantry that was in no way grotesque, bowed. He gave her the most direct look she had ever gotten from an unfamiliar man. It unnerved her. She uncrossed her legs.

"Would it be uncivilized of me," said Bevilaqua in his high-pitched voice, "to suggest again that we eat?"

"A very good idea," Minnie agreed. "Ah, but Fortunato hasn't met the guest of honor. Come and see my grandson."

There was no self-pity in Fortunato's manner when he said, "He can do without meeting me." By this time, he was standing under the archway between the kitchen and living room.

"But the baby's right here," Minnie said with a jerk of her

head in Stefano's direction. He sat placidly as ever on the drifts of pillows. Fortunato pointedly avoided looking at the child. Minnie took him by the hand. "Come." When they reached the couch she said. "Nice baby, no?"

He stole a look at the child and, after a small pause, said, "This baby is not very beautiful and not too lucky. He doesn't deserve so much attention."

Minnie was stunned. Cynthia and Ray were insulted. Aunt Angela muttered something under her breath.

Fortunato seemed to know what they were thinking. "If a child is praised too much," he explained, "jealousy is the result—and worse."

Arturo had been studying the scene with reflective puffs of a cigar. Behind the mist of smoke, his fathomless eyes narrowed. "Whom the gods would destroy," he said under his breath, "they would first raise up."

Minnie had regained her composure. "The celery soup is ready," she announced. "Fortunato, you sit next to Sister Anastasia, Father Mancuso, next to me where I can keep an eye on you, eh?" The priest's sad mouth turned up, and he sat where he was told to. All the others took their places.

Throughout the meal Arturo kept a watchful eye on Fortunato Ricci who sat to the right of the nun. She ladled his soup for him and paid him various motherly attentions which he accepted with no sign of interest. Every time Cynthia rose to clear away plates or help serve another course, Fortunato nailed her down obliquely with his crossed eyes. She broke a soup bowl.

Dr. Bevilaqua sucked up a strand of *maccheroni*, leaving a trail of tomato sauce on his chin. Ray was telling him of his plans to open a law office in the neighborhood providing inexpensive legal services for Little Italy. "I'll do civil work, criminal work. I'm gonna specialize in the working man and his family. The dons can get expensive lawyers from uptown."

Bevilaqua raised an eyebrow. "Don't turn away business. You have to live too. I wish some of the dons, as you call them, would bring their business my way." Bevilaqua was a member of an endangered species—the neighborhood general practitioner. And a good thing he had a passion for food, for he got paid more often in meals than in money.

When everyone had finished the pasta course, the men all lit up while the women cleared away the dishes. Except for the nun, who meditated before a tumbler of red wine.

Soon more food was piled on the table. The meat and vegetable pies were sliced and the vegetable dishes spread around. Then everyone burst into spontaneous applause at the grand finale.

Minnie carrying the ignominiously treated pig. He had an apple and two lemons in his mouth, and his butchered body sat on a bed of fresh spices. Snout charred, skin crackly brown. With the gestures of opera, she placed the platter in the center of the table. Eating resumed with noisy delight.

It was two hours before the coffee was poured. Arturo lit up another crooked cigar and leaned back in his chair to watch Fortunato. The dwarf was nibbling a piece of *pecorino* cheese with a look of vague distaste on his sallow face. He turned down a cup of coffee and Minnie frowned at his refusal, for it deprived her of a chance to bring pleasure.

Whenever Aunt Angela passed Fortunato's chair—as she did now on her way to the sink with a stack of dishes—she turned up her nose like she was passing a barrel of three-day-old fish. She moved with the shuffling gait of the very fat.

"This was a meal to remember," said Father Mancuso, raising a glass of Centerbe.

"God bless Stefano," Minnie responded, lifting a coffee cup.

Cynthia swirled mineral water in a wine glass. "I'll drink to that."

Fortunato's eyes leapt at her. He rose from his chair and walked around the table to the baby's highchair. His body had the grace of movement of a dancing crab. Everyone watched him as he stood directly in front of Stefano—luckless child before the graceful baby. Stefano made sounds at Fortunato, embryonic expressions of friendship.

Fortunato said not a word. He inserted his thumb between the first and second finger of the right hand and jabbed the air in a sexual gesture.

Priest and aunt, mother and grandmother were all horrified. In stunned silence they stared as Fortunato turned and walked silently out of the apartment. Only Arturo seemed unperturbed. Through clouds of cigar smoke, his dark, brooding eyes peered at the door Fortunato had closed behind him.

The guests all had left. Ray and Cynthia were asleep in Minnie's bedroom while Minnie's bedclothes were on the living-room couch. She sat in a chair by the open window, secretly smoking a filter cigarette and gazing into space. She was tired and troubled. A fluorescent lamp blinked out in the parking lot across the street. A fire engine whined and clattered down a nearby street. Minnie yawned distractedly.

Her stomach churned. Minnie had had this feeling before, this strange psychic call-to-arms. It seems she was predestined for life-and-death adventures. Conduct unbecoming a proper Italian Mamma. Something was happening again, she knew it. Something not very pleasant. And she would have to deal with it.

She sighed and rose from the rocker. It continued to sway in the breeze. Fear, an old companion, again walked with Minnie. She went over to the cradle and looked down at her sleeping grandson. His breathing was regular through the bud of his rosy mouth. Flashes of dreams registered in the twitching of his eyes. Minnie's heart swelled with emotion.

Then she noticed it. The amulet was gone.

Part Two
The Fascination

Chapter 10

Dr. Bevilaqua almost always wore sunglasses, an unofficial mark of professional status in the neighborhood. He took them off to peer with a pen light into the baby's mouth.

Cynthia sat back in a crimson armchair, crossed her legs, and bit noisily into an apple. She seemed unconcerned, even though for the third straight night Stefano had cried from dark till dawn. Minnie bit her lip anxiously and stood on tiptoe to gaze over Bevilaqua's pinstriped shoulder.

"He's okay, Doctor?"

Bevilaqua smiled. "I just began examining him." His tone was indulgent. "Have you taken his temperature?"

"Yes. He's slightly feverish," Cynthia replied. "What do you suppose it is?" She nibbled at the apple.

Bevilaqua shrugged and continued the examination. As the baby cried, he shone the light into his eyes and ears, then carefully examined all parts of his body. Gently, the doctor pressed on Stefano's abdomen. He showed no unusual reaction.

From his medical bag Bevilaqua produced a stethoscope and listened to Stefano's chest and back.

Minnie tried to read the doctor's bland expression as he took the instrument out of his ears and stuffed it back into the ragged black bag.

"Well?" she said impatiently.

Cynthia got up from the sofa, went over and picked up her wailing child. She rested him on her shoulder and walked around the room, patting him on the back and making comforting sounds. They waited for Bevilaqua's response.

He shrugged. "There's nothing wrong that I can see. I wouldn't worry about it. Probably a virus." He picked up his sunglasses and fitted them to his craggy face. His cheeks were slightly pitted with acne scars.

Minnie still looked anxious. "But why does he cry all the time?"

Bevilaqua smiled indulgently. "Because of discomfort. Babies have a low tolerance for such things."

Minnie could not shake her uneasiness. She knitted her brows and shook her head gravely. "It worries me."

"Ah, grandmothers," he said.

"Is there anything I should do?" Cynthia said, rocking the baby on her shoulder.

"Give him two baby aspirin before bedtime. I'll give you a special formula for his bottle."

"I breast-feed."

"Combine it with formula. But breast-feed before bed. It will soothe him." Bevilaqua picked up his bag and coughed.

Cynthia gave the baby to Minnie. "I'll write you a check, Doctor. How much?"

"Fifteen," he said, putting on his hat.

Cynthia looked mildly surprised. "That's very reasonable for a house call."

He chuckled. "I'm lucky to get that much in this neighborhood." He looked at Minnie. "I'd fiddle for my supper for this woman." He caught sight of the cradle by the open window. "The baby doesn't sleep there, does he?"

"Sure he does," Minnie said.

"That may be the problem. Move the cradle somewhere else."

"He can sleep in the same room as Ray and I," said Cynthia.

Minnie asked, "What's wrong with where he sleeps now?"

Bevilaqua formed a mock frown. "Evil spirits will get him."

Minnie raised her hand to her mouth. "Not even as a joke," she admonished him.

His face softened. "Don't worry so much, Minnie. He will be all right." He clapped shut his bag. "I have to be at the clinic in twenty minutes."

"I'll see you to the door," Minnie said.

"Needn't bother. After all these years, I know where it is."

"How is the Signora?" Minnie inquired, accompanying him anyhow.

"My wife is in constant good health," he said with a sour expression. "Her latest obsession is yoga. Whenever I come home, I never know what position I will have to get into to look her in the eye. She seems to spend more time on her head than a normal person spends on the seat of the pants."

Bevilaqua made a grand show of complaining about his wife, many years younger, Irish, and a schoolteacher. He was devoted to her.

On the way to the door Bevilaqua took the check from Cynthia and stuffed it into his jacket pocket without looking at it. He touched the brim of his hat. "Have a good weekend, ladies. Call me soon again if he shows no improvement."

Cynthia watched him depart with narrowed eyes. When the door had closed behind him, she said, "Evil spirits, my foot. Is the man a doctor or a witch doctor?"

Minnie looked sharply at her daughter-in-law. "He was

only joking." Her face darkened. "At least I hope so." She held the baby closer. He had stopped crying and was whimpering softly.

"*Povero bambino,*" she cooed. "Poor baby."

Cynthia strode across the room and picked up a pack of cigarettes from the end table near the couch. Deftly, she jostled the pack, made a slim cigarette jump up from the opening, and caught it with her long fingers. Her full red eyebrows came together as she lit up. "He just has a bug, Mamma. Don't fuss over him."

Minnie shook her head sagely. "You never know about these things. Especially in the first year of life. They are so delicate, so defenseless." Minnie remembered Romolo who died before he could live. Stefano drew his mouth down sadly, causing Minnie fairly to burst with sympathy. "Look at the way he pouts. Just like Remo used to do. Just like him. *Povero bambino.*"

Cynthia blew out a cloud of smoke. "What's keeping the famous co-founder of Rome anyhow? He should have been home an hour ago." Ray had gone to the bank to negotiate a loan to open his office and fix up the loft.

Minnie was getting angry. Must she speak always with sarcasm about her husband? "Maybe something came up. Maybe he needed to get another reference or something."

Cynthia languidly sat down on the couch. "Or something." She exhaled another gust of smoke and watched the plumes rise. The baby started to cry again.

"He could have called," Cynthia said.

Minnie looked anxiously at Stefano. "He's still in pain."

Cynthia frowned. "It's feeding time. Give here."

Meekly now, Minnie handed over the baby. "Shouldn't we try the formula," she suggested. "Doctor Bevilaqua said . . ."

"He's a quack. You said it yourself, there's nothing like mother's milk." She rested the baby in her lap, unbuttoned her blouse, unhooked the right cup of her bra, and took out her breast. In a second, Stefano's crying mouth was otherwise occupied.

"He looks hungry," Minnie said.

Cynthia continued smoking nonchalantly as the baby suckled noisily. Minnie looked away, thinking it unseemly for a mother to smoke and feed at the same time. Unhealthy, too. She was trying to like this woman for her son's sake. But she knew she didn't.

"Can I ask you a question?"

Cynthia looked up from a magazine. "Go ahead."

"Why did you take the necklace off when you said you wouldn't?"

"Necklace?"

"The coral amulet. Against *malocchio*."

"Oh, that thing. I didn't even notice it was gone."

"You're saying you didn't take it off?"

"That's what I'm saying. Maybe it fell off."

Minnie was silent. She wondered if Cynthia was telling the truth. She decided to press the issue. "It's funny you didn't notice it was gone. You bathe him all the time."

She didn't raise her eyes from the magazine. "It just didn't occur to me. I'd completely forgotten about that doodad."

Minnie frowned, puzzled. "What's a doodad?"

"A trinket."

"Oh," she said, still not understanding. She pondered a moment. "Maybe it did fall off. Maybe it did. But as soon as it was missing, Stefano started to get sick, you know that? As soon as it was gone."

Cynthia slammed the magazine down. "Oh, come on now."

"I'm not saying there's a connection for sure."

"I should hope not."

Just then Ray walked into the apartment, looking morose. He muttered a greeting and made straight for the refrigerator. "Hot in here. Why doesn't somebody turn on the window fan?"

"You didn't get the loan," Cynthia said.

He produced a cold chicken leg and shut the refrigerator door. "I got the loan." He bit into the chicken.

"Then why the long face?" asked Minnie.

"Cause now I'm in debt. Cause it's hot, cause the baby's sick. Ah, I don't know why." Chomping on the chicken leg, he went into the bedroom and slammed the door behind him.

Cynthia went back to her magazine and feeding the baby.

Minnie shook her head sadly. Inwardly, she found fault with Cynthia for being so unmoved by her husband's ill temper. But she said nothing.

Cynthia took the baby off the breast and stood up to burp him. Bouncing Stefano on her shoulder, she stooped to squash out the cigarette. "Let him sulk. Whatever's bothering him, he'll feel better if he's left alone."

Minnie shrugged and went into the kitchen. Outside the window, the declining day cast the surrounding tenements in umbral tones, and a full moon rose like a specter in the failing sunlight. She picked up the watering can and walked to her favorite plant, swaying in the lethargic breeze. She took in her breath sharply. Her beautiful, pampered Swedish ivy was dying.

Chapter 11

The door swung open to Arturo's ruddy face wearing a puzzled look, eyes squinting through gusts of cigar smoke at the unexpected caller on his threshhold. Then, recognition. "Minnie, *benvenuta,* my friend. Come in, please."
With a welcoming gesture he stepped aside and ushered her into his walk-up apartment, a place as shadowy as his personality. "Forgive the mess, I seldom have visitors." He noticed her appalled expression. "Ah, I know it looks dark and dreary, Minnie, but it suits me, yes it suits me well. You know, my ancestors in Matera were cave dwellers."
"In New York, we are all cave dwellers," Minnie said, stepping inside.
"You're right. But I carry it to an extreme. I'll brew some coffee." With a flurry of activity, he cleared newspapers off a ragged daybed and gathered up a plate and fork caked with egg. "Sit here. Make yourself comfortable."
Uneasily, she sat down. Minnie was very nervous. She knew times had changed and many things were considered ac-

ceptable now that weren't when she was a girl. Still, a southern Italian lady just did not go unescorted to a man's apartment. Otherwise, how could such a passionate race resist temptation? So the veil of formality should not be dropped. Yet Minnie had felt she had to come.

She looked around her. What a place! Although they had been friends for some six years now, Minnie had had no conception of how Arturo lived. It was a two-room apartment in the back. The single window looked out on alleyways, and the low floor and high adjoining buildings cut off practically all natural light. They were now in what might be called the living room, a small, cluttered cubicle with a pullman kitchen. A door off to the right led to what Minnie presumed was the bedroom. The walls, badly in need of paint, were green and blotched with water stains.

After he had puttered around the hot plate, Arturo sat in a shabby armchair opposite Minnie and smiled at her, trying to put her at ease. "The coffee will be ready in a moment. Please relax. Can I get you a piece of fruit or cheese?"

She looked demurely down at her hands folded in her lap. "No thank you. I am not hungry."

He sensed her awkwardness, and put his hand out to touch her wrist. She looked up at him. He smiled again, baring stained teeth. The top buttons of his yellowed white shirt were open, showing a hairless chest. He spoke to her in that peculiar voice of his, a voice without tone or sex: "Don't worry about anything. Especially not about appearances. I am too old, Minnie, and besides . . . " His voice trailed off into a chuckle. "Just don't worry, eh?"

She smiled back at him. "I'm not worried about anything." She looked around her again at his strange collection of things. A stuffed owl stared at her from atop a chest of drawers; old books wers strewn in crates he used as end tables. Mounted on the wall were the horns of an elk; candles fluttered in corners, and amid the debris prowled two cats and an Asiatic-looking mongrel.

The owl looked at Minnie reprovingly while a pompous Australian parrot screeched at her from a big cage hanging from the ceiling.

She shuddered. "The owl gives me the creeps."

"Does he? That's funny because you should feel utterly comfortable together. The owl was sacred to the goddess Minerva."

"What a strange place," she said candidly.

He laughed. "Yes. But it suits me, as I said. How are you, Minnie? How is your family?"

"The baby is sick."

He clucked his tongue. "The coffee should be ready."

Soon he returned with a tray holding two cups, silverware, napkins, Stella D'Oro biscuits and a small coffeepot. He placed the tray on the wooden table between them.

She asked him, "Do you really believe in the power of *malocchio?*"

"I forgot the milk and sugar." He returned with a carton of milk and a box of sugar. "I'm sorry I have nothing fancy to put them in." He served her. "I remember you take milk and two spoons of sugar."

She looked at him expectantly.

"I will answer your question in time. Let's just have our coffee. *Un biscotto?*" She took a biscuit and bit into it without enthusiasm.

When they had finished, Arturo methodically cleared the table and brushed off the crumbs while Minnie fidgeted. Finally, he said, "Come with me, Minnie." He walked toward the door to the other room.

Out of modesty, Minnie hesitated for a moment but she soon overcame her reluctance and followed him into the room. Her mouth dropped open. By comparison, the outer room was a model of tidiness and conventionality. It was not, as she had presumed, a bedroom but a kind of storeroom for Arturo's collection of oddities and amulets. From the doorframe hung branches of berries.

Arturo saw Minnie inspecting them. "Juniper," he said. "Against evil spirits. In Italy, our legends say that the Blessed Mother was hidden by juniper branches during the flight into Egypt."

From various sections of the ceiling strings of garlic and onion and sprigs of rue were suspended. On the far wall hung the skin of an animal, its fur tied with bright red ribbons. It looked like a wolf skin. Almost all of the walls were covered with something or other—horns of elks and oxen, tusks of wild boar, and a large shield embossed with Saint George slaying the dragon. Minnie gave a mild start when she turned toward another wall and stared straight into the eyes of the mounted head of a dog, its fangs bared. Arturo smiled and led her farther into the room which, deceptively, was twice the size of the other room, where he spent most of his time.

In the middle was a large wooden table covered with a black cloth and strewn with more paraphernalia, including two human skulls. Arturo picked up a wooden harlequin doll with a chain attached and handed it to Minnie. "Pull the chain." She pulled the chain and the legs and arms moved in different directions. "It baffles the evil eye."

Minnie put the doll down and her eyes swept the array of amulets—bracelets, necklaces, brooches, pins, and signet rings. How many shapes and forms! Lotuses, sea horses, crosses, keys, hearts, a key with a heart handle, cocks, serpents, eagles, fish, frogs, tortoises, scarabs, and phalluses. And they were made of many materials: silver, coral, gold, mother-of-pearl, bone, amber, lava, shells, and wood. There were cock spurs, claws of crabs and lobsters, claws and teeth of wolves and bears strung together. By far the most common were small horns or crescent moons of coral.

Minnie was breathless. "Where did you get all these?"

"Here and there over the years."

"Why?"

He showed his stained beaver teeth. "Shall I say it is my hobby?"

"Then you *do* believe in the *malocchio.*"

Slowly, he sat down on a burlap-covered chair, rested his freckled hands on his kneecaps, and looked directly at her. "I have seen it at work."

Minnie looked skeptical, but she was a religious woman of the sort who kept an open mind to spiritual wonders. She sat across from him in a leather armchair. "Tell me about it."

"What do you want to know?"

"Everything."

He laughed indulgently. "I don't know everything."

"Tell me what you know."

"One thing I know is that you too believe in the evil eye."

"I? I don't know if I do."

"Why are you here, then?"

"To investigate."

"A fair answer." He got up from the chair. "Do you believe in envy?"

"Of course."

He walked over to a bookshelf. "And you believe in the Holy Scripture?"

"Yes."

"The Bible calls envy an evil eye." He pulled a copy of the New Testament from the shelf. It was next to three other volumes, *Talks on Fascination, Commonly Called Throwing,* by Nicolo Valetta, *South Italian Folkways in Europe and America,* by Phyllis H. Williams, and *Malleus Malificarum,* Samuel Johnson's Dictionary. "In 'Saint Paul's Epistle to the Galatians,' he warns them of it."

"So the evil eye is the result of envy, you say?"

"The worst forms of it are invariably so. I explained it to you at the bingo game. You can be an involuntary thrower. That means somebody who casts the evil eye without really wanting to. Or you can be a voluntary thrower who casts the evil eye on purpose. From ill will. From envy."

"Who envies us?" Minnie had asked herself the question aloud.

Arturo said nothing to this. "Many casters are innocent," he continued. "The Church is right when She tells us that full intent of the will is a prerequisite for sin. The dogma is an acknowledgment that evil can be spontaneous. That sometimes nobody but evil personified can be blamed for a calamity.

"But many casters are not innocent. They have the choice not to exercise the power, yet they do it out of evil intent." From a sagging breast pocket he produced a packet of DeNobili cigars. He lit up and, with obvious pleasure, drank in Minnie's rapt expression.

"Envy," she said, drawing the word out meditatively.

He blew out his first gust of smoke and slipped the package back into his breast pocket. "What is our word for 'envy' in Italian?" he asked rhetorically. "*'Invidia'*—'a looking-into.' We look with our eyes, and sometimes they are evil eyes."

"So the only difference between a voluntary and an involuntary caster is intent."

"Correct. They have the same power." He flicked an ash. "Of course, there are minor forms of this art—or this affliction, however you see it." He snorted. "I'm sounding professorial."

She waved him away. "I'm learning a lot."

"Have you heard of the *'jettatore sospensiva'*? He is the thrower who makes you miss the train or brings rain to your picnic. He means well, but nobody wants him around. Involuntary type."

Minnie looked into the distance. "I knew a person like that when I was a girl. She was the tailor's wife in my village."

"They say Pope Pius the Ninth had the evil eye."

"Even priests?"

"Even the priest of priests. Involuntary, naturally." His wink was jaunty.

Minnie was almost enjoying this. "Is the evil eye a belief with other people?"

"Oh, many." He prefaced the next with a grin, "But we

Italians are the source of the river. The Irish call it 'the *maloik*,' you know."

"There's something fascinating about this subject."

He laughed heartily. "Apt word. The spell of the *malocchio* is called *'il Fascino'*—'the Fascination.' And the possessors of the power often are indeed fascinating, charming. They can literally charm birds out of trees. Literally. Cats have the power."

"Animals, too?"

"Certamente. I had a house cat when I was a boy in Matera . . ."

"I thought you said you lived in a cave."

"I said my ancestors did. I once saw this house cat—his name was Carminuccio—I once saw him stare a bird out of a tree. It fell to the ground as if hypnotized. Carminuccio nonchalantly walked over, picked the bird up in his mouth, and fastidiously went to a private place to eat him. The power."

"But Arturo, how can you know if you are afflicted by the evil eye?"

He grunted. "Good question. It's hard to tell."

"You're the expert. Tell me."

"I'm the expert. But if I knew the whole answer to the hard questions I would be a wizard, not an expert."

"Then tell me some of the answer."

"Why all the interest?"

"Tell me."

He nodded seriously. "There are symptoms." He wagged a finger at her. "Mind you, they could mean something else as well."

"I take the warning."

"Headaches, for example." He shrugged. "They *can* come from the evil eye, but they can come from lots of other things—general weakness, fatigue, a stomachache. An unpleasant sensation of warmth at the moment one is 'overlooked' or 'fascinated'. All have many other causes. Does that make this *malocchio* idea suspicious? Yes. Does it make it false? Who knows? Having considered many other sides of the matter, I have decided it is not false."

"What other sides? Tell me."

"It would take weeks."

"Start somewhere."

"Why the impatience?"

"Stefano."

"It's probably something else."

"But it may *not* be."

He grunted in agreement. "Why are you so quick to believe all this?"

"I don't know why. I don't know."

"I think I do."

She looked startled. "What makes you think so?"

"Your interest is natural. You're a witch, Minnie."

She looked positively aghast.

His mouth turned up. "Not a witch like with a broomstick, an ugly face, and a black hat. You're not an American witch. You're a *strega*. An Italian witch."

"That doesn't make me feel any better."

"That's because, like most people, you know little about witches. I know what I'm saying, you know little about your own kind."

"But if I am a witch . . . "

"It takes study anyhow. Don't worry, Minnie. You're a *strega benevola*. You're a good witch."

"Still . . . "

He looked mildly scornful. "It's not that you're some kind of ghost. You're a normal person. You're gifted, that's all. Be grateful for it."

She smiled and tapped her forehead. "Ah, you've almost got me believing all this."

He answered with a smile. "Why not? The witch is a respected figure. The *Napolitani* call her Ianara. It's the same as the goddess Diana. Minnie, you're like a goddess. Be proud."

She blushed. *"How* do you know I'm a witch?"

"It takes one to know one." The beaver teeth flashed again.

"But witches are women, aren't they?"

"Not all. Some witches are like angels. Sexless."

Minnie looked surprised.

"By the way," he said, "I am a good witch too. You and I have this in common: we have the evil eye in reverse. The *good* eye."

"I have so many questions. How do you spot a bad witch?"

"You know your natural enemy. It's instinctive."

"With animals, maybe," she demurred. "Not always with humans."

His nod granted the point.

"So how can you tell?"

"They are sometimes hard to pick out," he conceded. "Their skins can be camouflage. But often they are exactly what they appear to be. Obvious. That's what makes them hard to spot.

"Good witches can be male or female. The same with bad witches?" Minnie asked.

"The same. Bad or good, though, more witches are female than male. I don't know why."

Minnie went over to the table and picked up a necklace charm. "Is this real silver?"

"Uh-huh."

She inspected the round pendant closely. "How strange. Who is this creature with snakes in her hair?"

"A gorgon. A female monster."

"Of course," Minnie said with a start of recollection. "My father told me the story. Her name was Medusa."

"That's right. All men who looked upon her were turned to stone. The power."

"Medusa had the evil eye? But isn't this an amulet *against* the evil eye?"

"Ah, yes. The best way to combat the evil eye is to give the witch a taste of her own medicine. Anyway, that's the belief—or the superstition, if you see it that way."

"Like a mirror."

He blew out smoke and smiled approvingly. "Exactly. Fight evil with evil. But don't be the source of evil yourself. Turn the evil against itself. It fits in perfectly with the myth. Do you recall it?"

"Medusa was killed, wasn't she?"

He nodded. "By Perseus. Remember Cellini's statue of him? It is in Florence."

"I've never been to Florence."

"You should go someday. Perseus was clever. He borrowed a shield from the goddess Athena. It was polished brass, and in it he could see the reflection of the monster without meeting her eyes. He cut off her head and presented it to Athena."

Minnie fingered the charm. "You know your mythology."

He raised his eyebrows. "There are lessons within."

Still holding the necklace, Minnie sat down again. She looked at it for a while, then raised her anxious face to Arturo. "I want to know more. Are there ways to tell that the evil eye is coming? Omens?"

"Yes. But they are not foolproof." He laughed. "Ours is an inexact science."

"Tell me about them."

"I myself don't put too much stock in harbingers. But they say that you are forewarned if you see, say, a black cat, or a shaggy dog, or a deformed person, a squinter, or a barefoot woman. These are the main ones."

Minnie felt apprehension grow. She remembered her shopping trip on the day before Ray and his family came home. The cat in the alley and the barefoot girl she ran into outside the fish store. Then soon after, she talked to Fortunato.

"You'll think I'm crazy. I saw these things—on a day not long ago."

"I don't think you're crazy. But we must be careful. We often see such things and they mean nothing."

"All at the same time?"

"Not often. But memory can be . . . creative, let's call it."

"I saw a black cat, a barefoot girl, and Fortunato, all in the space of a few minutes last week. I recall it clearly."

He removed the cigar from his mouth and shrugged. "Maybe."

She shook her head vigorously. "Not maybe. Positively."

"Even so, it may not mean anything."

Her eyes burned with determination. Arturo knew that at the core of this pliant, yielding woman was steel.

"I must know for certain. You see, the baby is involved."

"What's wrong?"

"The doctor doesn't know. It's just that he cries all the time. Sometimes, day and night." Her eyes blinked rapidly. "He never used to cry at all. Never. Nobody seems very worried but me. But he used to be such a happy baby."

Arturo nodded. "You know, domestic animals, women, and children are most susceptible to the *malocchio*. Especially when they *are* healthy and beautiful."

Minnie nodded. "Beauty is the bane."

"Exactly."

"Is there something we can do?"

"What about the charm I gave him for his baptism?"

"It's gone."

"Missing?"

"Yes."

"His mother removed it?"

"She says she didn't. I don't believe her."

"Do you have reason not to?"

She shook her head. "I just don't."

"You don't like her."

"That's beside the point."

Cigar ash smoldered in a clam shell. He extinguished it with the butt and rose from the chair. "Don't worry. We will give him another amulet. The one you hold in your hand."

She looked at the face embossed on the pendant. It had a wild, intimidating expression. The eyes of the gorgon had no pupils and seemed to stare into eternity. "It is ugly."

He looked at it too. "You think so? I agree. It is a reflection of the evil it is designed to fight. We'll hang it on his crib."

"Is there any way to be certain about this evil eye?"

"No. But we'll try a method of diagnosis in any case. Can you arrange for us to be alone in the house with the baby?"

"I'll get Ray and Cynthia to go to a movie. They like to get out of the house."

"Good. As soon as possible."

"Maybe tomorrow. What will we do?"

"You'll see. You'll learn much and someday you will be the neighborhood healer."

"Me? I'm content to be a grandma."

"You're special, Minnie. You can't escape it."

Minnie felt pride and apprehension. The blank eyes of the gorgon challenged her. Arturo had walked over to her. He put his hand on her shoulder and she looked up from the amulet. "There's nothing special about me," she said, doubt edging her voice. "I'm like so many other women."

"Are you sure?"

"Of course."

He was silent for a moment. "After Perseus decapitated the Medusa, he gave the head to the goddess Athena. From that moment on it appeared on her shield, on most of her statues. It became the main symbol associated with her."

She scoffed. "I am a good Catholic."

"So what? There is no contradiction. Someday you will understand."

The amulet felt cold in her palm.

"In mythology," he continued, "Athena was sort of a good witch. Do you remember the name of the Roman counterpart to the Greek goddess Athena?"

She raised a puzzled face to him. "No, I don't."

"Minerva, Minnie."

Chapter 12

Clouds grazed the outline of Minnie's apartment building. Arturo blinkered his eyes with his hand and looked up at the third-floor window where the American and Italian flags fluttered side by side. "Minootch," he hollered.

She appeared at the window and waved him up.

He scaled the stairs, a daily exercise that kept his legs strong. He passed cacophonous radiators and cracked plaster and heard the voices and music from other apartments. He reached the landing and knocked lightly.

Minnie opened the door. "Come in, Arturo. The baby is sleeping peacefully for once."

He removed his hat, baring his bald head. "Good. They are gone?"

"Since this morning. They jumped at the chance to have lunch in Chinatown and go to the movies."

"First we'll hang the juniper berries above the doorways."

"All of them?"

"Yes. A little bit on all of them. Do you have a stepladder?"

"No."

"Then give me a chair sturdy enough to stand on."

She nodded and went into the kitchen, returning a few seconds later with an oak chair. She set it down under the archway near the front door. "You know, I can't believe Fortunato would want to harm Stefano."

He stood on the chair and tied the berry branch to an electrical wire. "I don't think Fortunato is the one."

"But you once said . . . "

He bit his tongue in the concentration of attaching the berries. "There. I thought so at first. But not after the baptism party."

"Then who could it be?"

"Caution now. It may not be the *malocchio*. And if it is, the *jettatore* could still be Fortunato doing things to throw us off the track. But I don't think so."

"I'm confused."

He climbed down from the chair. "I don't blame you. Let's do the doorway to the bedroom." He carried the chair over, stood on it, and began attaching another branch. "Remember when Fortunato disparaged the child?"

"He can be sour sometimes."

"Disparagement is a way of avoiding the evil eye, not casting it. Praise leads to envy." He got down from the chair. "Yet he may be a devious thrower, trying to avoid suspicion. He certainly has reason to be envious of that beautiful baby. Now the kitchen."

She followed him. "But when he made that awful gesture."

"*La fica,* yes."

She blushed at the obscenity.

He broke off another branch of berries and climbed up on the chair again. "That is a gesture against the evil eye." He climbed down and appraised his work. "The juniper is up. Let's hang the Medusa on the crib."

"If it's not Fortunato, then who *is* the *jettatore?*"

"Or *jettatrice*," he said solemnly. "The thrower might be a woman. Remember still, it may not be the *malocchio*."

They went into the bedroom and he turned to Minnie. "You have it?"

She nodded and produced the necklace from her apron pocket. She held it out to him.

"Hang it on the crib."

"How do I attach it?"

"Tie it to that piece of wood sticking out on top. Make sure it's fastened securely."

Doing so, she said, *"Se malocchio non ci fosse."*

Inserting his thumb between two fingers, Arturo jabbed the air and said in dialect, *"Te faccio na fica. Mal uocchie non ce pozzano.* May the evil eye not touch you."

"I hope it does some good."

He shrugged. "These are preventive measures. If he is already afflicted, they will not help much. Have you some coffee?"

In the kitchen, they drank in moody silence. Suddenly Minnie asked again, "Who is the witch?"

"You are quick to believe."

"I have a feeling. Who can it be?"

He looked at the window. "Your plant is dying."

"I know. Who?"

"An envious person. There are many. Somebody who had a chance to gaze on the baby."

"Somebody who came to the party?"

"There were many in church too. Maybe it was somebody we didn't even see. That plant was always healthy, wasn't it?"

"Who, who?"

He drained the cup. "Let us do a test."

"The diagnosis?"

"Yes. Bring me water in a basin and olive oil."

She went to a cupboard and got a can of olive oil and a deep bowl. She set them on the table before him. He instructed her,

"Open the door to the bedroom. The baby must be part of this."

"Shouldn't we perform it in there?"

"That's not necessary. He's close enough. Pour a big cup of water into the bowl."

Minnie poured, then looked at him, her eyes glowing with expectation.

"Get a spoon and let three drops of oil fall onto the surface of the water."

"Me? No, you do it."

"Minnie, you must learn to do these things."

"I don't want to."

"I will do it." He frowned. "But remember the way it's done."

Slowly, with an air of ceremony, he dropped the oil into the water. They watched as two drops merged into one and the third stood alone.

Arturo grunted with disappointment.

"What does it mean?"

He shook his head. "It's uncertain. If all three drops had formed a single circle, it would definitely mean the evil eye. If all three drops had stayed apart, it would mean the evil eye is not the cause. But this way, we still don't know."

She urged him, "Do it again."

"It wouldn't help. The ceremony cannot be repeated. It would tell us nothing."

"But we *must* know."

"That is the way it is. We are not meant to know now. We can do nothing about it."

The baby began to cry. Minnie looked anxiously at Arturo. "He's awake."

"So I hear. I have to go. Be patient. We will work on this together. Two good witches should be strong enough, once you learn the way."

"Leave me out of this witch business."

"Don't you want to help your grandson?"

"Of course. But I am not a witch."

"Then call it healer."

"I am not a doctor."

"In your way you are, Minnie."

"How do you know?"

He rose from the chair and so did she. "There are many ways to tell. For one thing, you are the mother of twins. A good witch is often the mother of twins."

"Old country nonsense," she protested with a vigorous shake of her head.

"Is it?"

"He is only a little sick. Everything will be all right."

"I hope so." He reached into his pocket. "Take this. Put some into his milk."

She examined the herb. "What is it?"

"*Na cima di ruta,*" he said, over the whimpers of the baby.

"A sprig of rue."

"I don't know if I believe in these things, but I know that they cannot hurt. If they all work, he will be well protected."

"They are minor remedies and preventatives. There are more powerful things, if need be."

She accompanied him to the door. They could hear the baby whimpering now. Arturo held a pork-pie hat in his hands, revolving it slowly by the brim. "Stay in touch. I want to know how things are going."

"Of course."

He looked around him and suddenly spat on the floor. "Against the *malocchio.*" He put on his hat, tipped it, and departed.

Chapter 13

A bravura sun reared at noon over treeless White Street. Mopping his brow with a handkerchief, Ray walked past the old wooden porticos of the textile warehouses until he came to the corner building. There it was, the Lolita Lounge.

The bar was housed on the ground floor of a freshly painted three-story tenement. A hand-lettered sign read: TOPLESS BARMAIDS. A crimson curtain blocked his view. He frowned and reached for the gilt doorknob.

Behind the door, the sunny day dissolved into honky-tonk chiaroschuro. The jukebox thumped out rock music and the place teemed with lunch hour customers. Stock clerks, civil servants, truckers, and Wall Street office workers draped themselves over the twenty-foot bar. Two girls worked the bar and one waited tables. He spotted her. She was the one at the far end of the bar beneath the blinking beer sign.

She was chatting with two customers wearing suit jackets and the forced smirks of sexual banter. Her pearly complexion was bathed in red light. She still wore her hair pulled back severely to highlight prominent cheekbones and keen features, and she had hauteur written all over her beautiful face. Outwardly, at least, she hadn't changed. He swallowed hard and began to walk toward her.

She was wearing practically nothing—high heels, bikini pants, and a diaphanous "baby doll" top that clearly exposed her large breasts and upright nipples. She had her hands on her hips and her bottom resting on a stool. He elbowed a space at the bar. The reflex smile she reserved for new customers appeared on her face for a split second, then vanished.

"Hello, Valentina."

She covered her surprise with insolence. "What'll it be?" she said sharply.

"I want to talk to you."

"What'll it be?"

"Beer."

"Imported or domestic?"

"Got Heineken?"

"Becks."

He nodded.

She turned to get a bottle from the cooler. His gaze moved down the curve of her back to the swell of her buttocks. In one fluid motion, she uncapped the bottle and placed it with a glass on the bar before him. "Two bucks."

He threw down a crumpled ten. After she gave him his change, she turned and resumed her conversation with the two men.

"Hey," he said.

The men gave him icy stares. "Be right back," she told them. She got up from the stool and walked over to him. "What can I do for you now?" she drawled.

"Can't we talk?"

She gave him a withering look. "You don't buy any privileges with one beer."

"Even at two bucks a throw?"

She pointed her breasts at him. "You can always take your business elsewhere."

"Tina . . ."

"What do we have to talk about?"

"Plenty."

"Sure. We can compare notes on marital bliss."

"This place, Tina."

"Now don't give me the Virgin Mary rap. I got work to do."

"It's not prudery. You're too good for it."

"I know. You're gonna take me away from all this. Listen, I got paying customers."

She started to turn away and he touched her wrist. "Come on. Give me a few minutes. Just a few."

A crack appeared in the iceberg expression. "After the lunch rush." She picked his hand off her wrist and dropped it like a dead eel. "A few minutes."

He studied the foam in the beer as she went back to the customers. The jukebox pounded in his ears. He looked up and scanned the room. The barmaid at the other end was a short Latin type in a black bikini. Her breasts were enormous. He slugged his beer.

Three bottles and ninety minutes later, they were sitting at a rear table. She ate a plate of Nova Scotia salmon with dry white wine. A fourth bottle of beer stood before him.

"I bring my lunch in from Balducci's," she informed him. "All you can get here is a sausage hero and Gallo red."

"That doesn't sound bad."

"Not every day, Garibaldi, not every day." She ate with obvious hunger. "So what's on your mind?" She picked up a slice of rye bread, smeared it with butter.

"I wanted to see you."

"Get an eyeful?"

"Tina, what's happened to you?"

She met his gaze directly. His gray eyes bored into her, but she didn't flinch. Finally, her long lashes dropped toward the pink salmon. "I'm doing research for a Ph.D. thesis."

"Are you still married?"

She covered a slice of bread with smoked fish and raw onion. "What are you? From the welfare department?"

"Valentina, I care about you."

She swallowed a bite. "As usual, you reek of nobility. I'm doing just fine."

His eyes narrowed. "I didn't know you disliked me this much."

Her silence affirmed it.

"I heard you got married when you came back from Chicago."

"You heard right." She drained the wine glass and poured another glassful.

"Why? You hardly knew him."

"It was fashionable. How's the belle of Baton Rouge?"

He grimaced. "Fine."

"Sued you for divorce yet?"

"We have a baby—a boy."

Color drained from her face. "I know."

"And you?"

"Nick is rich, good-looking, and about as exciting as a two-dollar haircut. I walked out on him."

"Divorced?"

"Nothing legal. I just moved out."

"Where are you living?"

"Around here. With a roommate."

"Why didn't you go back to modeling? You had such a promising career. And what about your plans to be an actress?"

"I decided they were frivolous, materialistic pursuits. I preferred to work for the betterment of mankind, so I became a topless barmaid. Someday, if I work hard enough, I may become a bottomless barmaid. Next question?"

Minnie Santangelo and the Evil Eye

"Can we be friends?"
"You mean you want to get laid."
"Don't be ridiculous."
"Don't give me that wounded look."
"Why can't we be friends?"
"Because I hate your guts," she said through her teeth.
"You don't."
Her eyes burned into him.
He dropped his gaze. "Maybe you do, at that."
She studied his face, cropped brown hair curling in tight sprigs over his bony forehead, nose with slightly deviated septum, square jaw and cleft chin. "I've hated you ever since you threw me over. I'm not the forgiving type, remember. I'm Sicilian."
"It wouldn't have worked between us."
"How did you find out about my gig in this place?"
"Heard about it in the neighborhood. It upset me very much."
She clucked her tongue. "You're such a sensitive soul, Father Santangelo."
"You have to quit this job."
"Listen, you ginny bastard, I like it here. Now buzz off."
"Why get angry? If we ever meant anything to each other, you must . . ."
"Why did you marry that skinny bitch?"
"Please, Tina . . ."
The girl who waited tables came over. She was a hard-looking bleached blond with very white skin and heavy thighs. "This dude hassling you, Tina?" Ray looked up at her. Her face was a red smear of lipstick and false eyelashes. Her splayed nipples bobbed before his eyes. She waited for an answer.
"Never mind, Beth," Tina finally said. "I can handle him."
"Whistle if you need anything." She turned and, with a

clatter of gold pumps, walked to another table. Ray watched the weight shift on her ass and then let his gaze return to Valentina's lovely face, illuminated by a soft light from overhead. She was like a finely cut diamond in a rhinestone setting. He couldn't help himself, "Tina, you just don't belong here."

She looked at him through the smoke and haze. "You haven't answered my question. Why did you marry her?"

He made a tent with his hands and stared at it. "Sometimes I wonder."

"You don't love her?"

He took a slug of beer straight from the bottle. "We get along fine."

"That's not what I asked."

"Sure I love her."

"That didn't sound too convincing."

"It's the emotion that gives me doubts, not the person."

"You bastard. You don't love anybody."

"Do you love your husband?"

"Let me count the ways." She held up the fingers of her right hand, then dropped them in disgust.

"Why did you marry him?"

"For money."

"Then why don't you collect alimony? You never cared for money. Why did you marry him?"

"You know the answer."

"Tell me."

"Okay, if I have to spell it out. I was his ricochet baby, you bastard." She yelled across the room. "Beth, would you bring me a Remy Martin?"

"Did he know?"

"He didn't care. I wore him for a pinky ring. He'd take me back tomorrow under any conditions. Nick Hampton is as soft as a sponge. And he's got just about as much character as one, too." She stole a look at him and her face softened. "We would have made quite a pair, you and I. A textbook romance."

"It would never have worked."
"Is it working now?"
"We have a son."
"I wanted your son. I feel like killing that bitch."
"You don't even know her. You never even saw her."
"You sure of that?"
The clack of high heels. Beth set down the cognac and melted back into the crowd.
"What do you mean?" he asked her.
She sipped the drink. "Forget it."
"You wouldn't be working here if your uncle were still alive."
"He couldn't control me either."
"No, but he'd have had the joint closed down."
"Well, Bert Marrandino ain't alive. So much for academic discussions."
"Can't I convince you to do something better with your life?"
"Why don't you split? What's your scam, anyhow? You're not my godfather."
"Look, I can't stand seeing you do this to yourself."
"Fuck off."
He looked around at the men in the place, nursing their beers and their noontime fantasies. "You want these dunces ogling you all day? That make you feel valued? Come on, don't throw away your future. There's only one to a customer."
"It's mine to squander if I like. Think about your own life."
"I think about it plenty. Like I said, though, I care about you."
"Don't be too sure you've got such a bright future. You and your lovely little family."
"Don't, Tina."
She brushed a wisp of hair back from her forehead, looked up from her cognac and searched his eyes. "Want to come to my place tonight?"

He held her gaze. "Thought you said you hated me."
"I do."
He dropped his eyes. "No thanks."
She finished off the cognac. "You want to. You want to real bad."
"I don't."
She snickered. "Bull shit. She doesn't do it for you, does she?"
"You're not going to sucker me into discussing this."
"We're too much alike, you and I. That's why you dumped me."
"It's not that way."
She leaned back in the chair and her naked breasts reared proudly. "You want to fuck me."
"I only want to see your life straightened out."
"You can taste it."
"No."
"I'm listed. On North Moore Street."
"You often sleep with guys you hate?"
"All the time."
"I'll bring my whip."
"*I* wield the whip."
"You never used to."
"Progress. Coming tonight?"
"No."
"You'll come. If not tonight . . ."
"No. Tina this isn't what I came here to talk about."
"I gotta go back to work."
He finished his beer. "Work," he said in disgust.
"Work is ennobling."
He got up from the chair. "Will I see you again?"
"Like I said, I'm listed."
"Will you talk to me, at least?"
"Sure." She assumed a mock leer. "Come up and see me sometime. But leave your social-worker badge at home."

Minnie Santangelo and the Evil Eye

He shook his head in exasperation, turned on his heel, and walked out into the radiant sunlight. With a bemused expression, she watched him leave. *That skinny bitch will be sorry,* she said to herself. *She'll be as sorry as a woman can be.*

Chapter 14

September arrived the next day in an ill temper. It was early morning, unseasonably cold, and a wind, high and irascible, whined through the streets of Little Italy. Baby Stefano had been coughing and crying almost all night long.

From the couch where she slept, Minnie could watch through the kitchen window the dawn streaking the sky with a fiery brush. She had slept only fitfully, and although the baby was quiet now she decided to get up.

She dragged herself into the kitchen and quietly made coffee. After taking turns sitting up with Stefano, Cynthia and Ray had finally drifted off into sleep. Minnie drank the first cup of coffee in three gulps and, impatient for the stimulant to take effect, poured another. She sat at the kitchen table moodily, until shafts of sunlight appeared on the vinyl tablecloth.

After a third cup, she pulled on some clothes and nudged open the bedroom door. They were all still asleep, but the baby was whimpering. Minnie looked worried. She closed the door and went back into the kitchen.

Yesterday they had summoned Bevilaqua again and he said

that the baby had an upper respiratory infection. The flu. Is the virus an evil spirit? Or the bacillus? Minnie could not answer these questions but she felt in her gut that there was something terribly wrong with her grandson.

Minnie knew this much: a baby cries either because he wants something or because he is in pain. Stefano had everything he wanted, so he must be in pain. And pain was a signal that he was being attacked by something. *What?*

She went to a kitchen cupboard and got out the pack of cigarettes she had hidden behind the demitasse cups. Smoking was her secret vice, a habit she resorted to infrequently, usually when she was very tense. Neither her late husband nor her son had ever seen her smoke, and she would be mortified if Ray ever caught her. In fact the only person who had ever seen her smoke was Angela, who smoked long, scented filter tips herself.

She lit up and blew out the smoke without inhaling. She doused the wooden match with tap water and put the evidence in the trash can.

Puffing nervously, she sat down to her coffee again. She was reminded of a conversation with her father in her native village of Penne long years ago. He was a burly schoolmaster with a handlebar mustache and a taste for alcohol and philosophic discourse. She imagined him raising and lowering his bushy brows as he talked, with a glass of *grappa* in his hand.

They were in the kitchen, warming themselves by coals burning in an earthenware pot. He leaned on his cane and smiled at his saucer-eyed daughter. "Have you ever heard of bacteria?" he asked her. He waited until she shook her head, even though he knew she hadn't. "Ah, they are tough little creatures who have been fighting and killing men for all time. You can't see them, except with an instrument called a microscope, but they are there waiting to invade the body, enter the blood and feed and multiply. They make poison, they hurt and sometimes they kill."

Minnie was nine years old. Her hazel eyes widened. "They are very bad things."

"They can be very bad."

"Did Satan make them and send them to us?"

He drank, and drops of *grappa* glistened on his mustache. "Some people think of it that way. But didn't God make Satan in the first place? Good and evil are so mixed up in this world. You know, sometimes we give these little devils to each other in acts of love. Diphtheria can come from a kiss."

Minnie's mother had been kneading dough for *maccheroni* on the table. She frowned in disapproval. "Shame. You shouldn't speak to her of such things at her age."

His eyes burned angrily. "The earlier we learn about life, the greater advantage we have."

The woman plunged her hands into the flour and muttered under her breath. She knew she was no match for him in debate.

Giorgio Monfalcone's eyes softened as they fastened on the face of his adoring daughter. "Yes, Minerva, we can mean well and hurt each other," he continued. "Bad can come from good. We injure while we nourish. We can catch an infection suckling the breast."

"How can the bacteria be so strong if they are so little?" Minnie asked.

His face lit up. "The question of a born philosopher. Nature is ingenious. Their very simplicity and small size make them strong. Millions of them can be carried by one tiny fly. You can catch a fever from the *saliva* of an insect. And they reproduce themselves at a fantastic rate."

"They are all around us. I will dream of them."

Lucia Monfalcone placed her hands on her hips. "You see what you're doing!"

"Quiet," he said sharply. "When we finish talking, she will not be afraid." He turned again to his daughter. "Bacteria can be used for good purposes, too. And there are ways to fight the bad ones. They are strong. But man may be stronger."

"How are they good?"

"Without some kinds, we would die. They enter our bowels at birth to help our bodies work. They make our provolone ripen and our wines ferment. And when we can't use them for our own ends, when they endanger us, we have been as ingenious as Nature herself. We kill them."

"How?"

He chuckled and drank from the glass. "In a clever way, a very clever way." He dabbed his mustache with his hand. "We make something called a vaccine. We grow these little devils in a test tube and then we inject them into sick people and it makes them immune. It's a way of making them kill each other. Fight fire with fire."

Minnie drew on the cigarette. It was just like Arturo had said, "Fight evil with evil." Like killing the Medusa with her reflection in the shield—with her own face on the amulet. "Give the witch a taste of her own medicine."

Minnie heard someone stirring in the bedroom. She quickly squashed the cigarette out in her saucer and brushed the butt and ashes into the trash can. Cynthia came into the kitchen.

"Good morning," Minnie said. Her face froze at her daughter-in-law's expression.

"Get the doctor, quick," said Cynthia.

Bevilaqua walked in under the juniper berries with his medical bag and a reassuring smile. Within five minutes the smile had vanished. He was examining the naked baby on Minnie's bed. Minnie, Cynthia, and Ray hovered over him. He addressed the child's mother. "When did you first notice the rash?"

"This morning."

Bevliaqua gently took the baby's head and tried to make his chin touch his chest. The baby howled. He couldn't do it.

"What is it, Doctor?" Ray asked as calmly as he could.

Bevilaqua shook his head and made for the phone. "We must get this child to a hospital."

Cynthia's hand clutched her mouth. She began to tremble. "My baby. What's the matter with him? My baby. Oh, what's the matter with my baby?"

Minnie went ice cold. She centered on the ingot of steel inside herself.

Bevilaqua dialed Saint Vincent's and reserved a bed for the child. Ray ground his teeth, balled his fists. "Come on, Bevilaqua, what the hell's wrong with him?" he shouted.

"I'm not positive."

"Tell us now," Ray yelled over his wife's sobbing and the baby's wailing. "Get it over with."

Bevilaqua threw him a veiled look, then met the young man's eyes directly. Expressionlessly he said, "Meningitis."

Cynthia buried her face in her hands and sobbed louder. Minnie crossed herself. Ray stood stock still and stared down at his son.

The doctor touched his shoulder. "My car's outside. Now let's get him to the hospital."

The second day of September mellowed. Summer returned, repentent and ardent. Tourists took refreshments under Campari umbrellas at the sidewalk cafés of Mulberry Street. Artists' wives bought mandarin oranges at the fruit stands of Mott Street. Kids spun and double-pumped on the playground courts while old men snoozed on the benches under a benevolent sun. And the baby died at Saint Vincent's Hospital.

Part Three
The Good Witch

Chapter 15

All day long, mosquitos sang their malarial madrigals near the fountain of Montevecchio. The sun sank and a wind came to the square, routing the insects and powdering the statue of Vittorio Emmanuele II with a coat of dust. Eva watched the poplars bend on the desolate western landscape and clutched the baby closer. The bus arrived and they got on.

Vesuvius loomed, a dramatic marking of the distant terminal. Through the window, cypresses fled backward, running home with Eva's heart. Green mold on the passing stone walls of the village, then the rutted road to Naples, to Carlo Levi's "Capital of the Poor." The bus clattered toward this squalid oasis. Eva was taking the deformed child to America.

Using foothill roads, the bus cut across Italy's twisted vertebrae, the Apennines, and soon the passengers caught a whiff of the sea. The baby had been sleeping soundly for three hours. As he stirred, a wing fluttered in Eva's breast. She cradled the flawed baby in her arms and crooned, "I am your mother now." The bus shambled over the despoiled countryside.

The peasant sitting next to them wore a beret, smelled of tobacco blended with manure, and snored in his sleep. Eva, who had spent most of her years in a *borghese* home, sniffed her irritation, placed the baby on her shoulder, and reached into her basket for dried figs and a narrow-necked bottle of wine.

First she fed herself and then she nursed the baby. She smiled to herself. How surprised they had been when she lactated. It was the thing that finally convinced them to give the child to her. At first the old lady, strong in family feelings, resisted the idea. Until Eva showed her she could give milk and begged to have the baby.

Eva's lactation had astounded all the villagers but a few crones who had heard of other cases. Simonetta was even called in again, to determine whether Eva was or had been pregnant, and how milk came to a barren girl. In a sun-drenched upper room Simonetta examined her and found nothing to explain it. She showed no surprise, though, and told the family that the girl was "a mother in sympathy."

The family pulled strings in Naples and Rome to identify Eva and the baby as brother and sister and get them visas for America. They would live at a Catholic welfare home in New York. It was all set within five months, great speed by local standards. And now they were actually on their way. The real mother, after her first look at the baby, never saw him again. They told her he was dead.

Eva pushed a lock of hair away from her cheekbone and took another long pull on the wine flask. The bus passed a shuttered hunter's cottage just visible in the dim light of the moon. A dog bayed in the encroaching forest as the bus went on.

They were nearing Naples, their waystation. In about three days they would embark to begin a new life. Steerage and the

Minnie Santangelo and the Evil Eye

Lower East Side, the noisy beat of life. Eva sighed and was happy in her way. Hope muted her inborn fatalism. Her finger traced the baby's soft cheek, and as she stared at the firegod Vesuvius rearing in the north, she wondered what was in store for them on planet America.

Chapter 16

There was a black-bordered photo of baby Stefano taped to Minnie's dresser mirror. She was profligate with her grief. She wept upon the flowers in the funeral parlor and ate dirt at the cemetery. She was strong enough to hold nothing in.

Then for three days after the funeral, she was numb. Cynthia flew to Baton Rouge to embrace her own mother and Ray got drunk every day. Minnie hardly cared. Numb.

Anger came next. Anger at Doctor Bevilaqua who might have saved Stefano's life, anger at Cynthia for not having taken the illness seriously enough, anger at Arturo for his skepticism, anger at herself for her powerlessness, and anger at her own cherished faith. She did something during this firestorm of anger that would have been incredible a week before. She deliberately shattered a plate bearing a picture of the Sacred Heart.

Finally she collapsed in a fit of sobbing. Arturo was there. He clasped her heaving shoulders. "Why did God do this to me?" Minnie asked. "What good were all those prayers I always said?"

Arturo wore a sympathetic frown. "Remember, Minnie, amen means 'so be it.' We end each prayer with a vow of acceptance. Accept it, Minnie. Accept it."

Her shoulders stopped heaving. She grew more tranquil. "Why did the priest not say such things to me?"

"I am your priest, Minnie."

She looked at him questioningly.

"If you let this thing beat you," Arturo said, "you won't have the strength to do what must be done."

"What?"

"Fight this evil eye."

Chapter 17

His bloodshot eyes made a sullen sweep of the Lolita Lounge, finding her at the near end of the bar, her acorn nipples and sulfurous glance. He steadied himself and tried to saunter over. Stumbled. He didn't care.

A necklace of shells rode the swell of her breasts. Underneath the artful makeup, her proud Sicilian face showed wary sympathy. Still, she faced down his defiant look.

"Ray," she said softly. Three customers turned to appraise him.

He stared back until they shifted their gazes. He sat on the barstool and let his bony shoulders slump under the soiled denim shirt. The others had gone back to drinking and talking. He sighed, inhaling the anesthesia of self-indulgence, exhaling a redolence of alcohol and sleeplessness. Three days' growth covered his sallow face and his gray eyes had lost their natural light. "Tequila," he said.

Tina poured the shot and wordlessly placed the glass before him. He peeled off a wrinkled five-dollar bill.

"Free ride," she offered.

His eyes clicked over her exposed flesh. "I'll pay," he announced theatrically.

Her mouth tightened. "It's your money. Salt and lemon?" she asked.

Without answering, he belted back the tequila and shoved the glass forward for a refill. She poured, breasts bobbing under hoisted elbow. Again she made change, then raised a solicitous face to him. "I'm sorry, Ray."

He grunted and drank.

"I know nothing I say can help. But I'm sorry."

"Let's have another drink."

She poured. "Shouldn't you go easy?"

"Fuck you."

This was overhead by a burly trucker, sipping sherry. His eyes questioned Tina, but she waved him away.

"Anything I can do?" she asked Ray.

He looked up from his glass. "Does the offer still hold?"

She looked bewildered.

"The offer to have sex with me," he slurred.

Now she was the one to look disapproving. "At a time like this?"

"What better time?"

"Sleep it off."

"I will. In your bed."

"Go somewhere else for your grudge fuck."

He leaned back on the stool for a panoramic view. "I want your bitch body."

"How boring."

"Your tits are hanging out," he said.

"Go home. Huh?"

"I wanna bury myself in ya."

"I'm not a crypt."

"You are."

"You're morbid, Ray. Your son dies and you wallow in it. Go home and grow up."

He flinched. "What'm I supposed to do? I can't fight it, I'll join it."

"You're a turncoat," she snarled. "You ought to fight it like your partisan ancestors. Death is a dictator too."

He waved his hand in disgust. "I could fight my own death, but my child died and the tyrant reigns forever." He swallowed the flames of tequila. "I'm going over to his side."

She surrendered to his ravaged eyes. "I'll sleep with you."

"When?"

"Whenever you say."

He put down the glass.

"It means my job."

His eyes scorched.

"I'll be dressed in five minutes," she said.

Chapter 18

Pursing her mouth, Minnie inspected the Swedish ivy. The leaves curled like parchment. She showed no remorse as she dumped it into the trash can. She placed the empty pot on the window sill and faced Arturo. "Is the coffee okay?"

"Just fine," he said, taking another sip to reassure her.

She yearned for a cigarette but wouldn't smoke in front of a man. Still frowning, she said, "I would have made it fresh."

"It's perfectly good warmed up," he said with a broad display of buck teeth. "Good to the last drop, like they say."

With a serious look, she sat down across from him.

It had been two weeks since the baby's funeral and a full week since they had seen each other. Arturo studied his friend's drained and pallid face. She looked a little better. He dunked a biscuit in his coffee. The seams in his face deepened as he chewed, waiting for her to speak.

"I'm ready," Minnie said.

He swallowed a morsel and cleared his throat. "Ready for what?"

"To do what must be done."

Arturo's expression showed satisfaction. He fiddled with the handle of the demitasse cup while a tiny smile flickered. "I knew you'd come around. This thing is in your blood, you know. In your nature."

"I'm ready to fight. To take revenge."

"You are convinced now of the evil eye?"

She nodded firmly.

"What convinced you?"

"Just something inside me. It killed my grandson. I know it."

"It isn't revenge you want."

"Yes, it is," she said stubbornly. She folded her arms, showing dimpled white elbows. "I want to get back at that witch."

"It's your duty, of course. But revenge has a bitter aftertaste. You'll see."

"In my youth, I lose a baby. In my old age, I lose another. In between, I lose a husband. What is this, anyway? I want revenge."

He lit a cigar, blew the match out. "You want to take charge, that's what you want. I don't blame you. But revenge? On who?"

"On the witch."

"God took your grandson."

"The Devil took him."

Arturo shurgged and flicked an ash. "Maybe so. He was only doing his job."

"I want retribution," she insisted.

Arturo's eyes brightened in their hollows and he bared his teeth. "Ah, yes. You deserve to be paid back. That's something different." He exhaled a gust of smoke and leaned back with an air of importance, a sage in a frayed-collar shirt. "You have to combat the evil force. It's your duty."

"My duty?"

"Your duty as a healer. As a good witch."

She shrugged her shoulders under the paisley print of her

housedress. "Give it a title, if you want. All I know is, my blood is boiling with the desire to get this witch." She frowned. "And I can't sleep."

"Don't worry, Minerva. Insomnia will pass when you win the fight."

Shyly, she touched his hand. "What am I supposed to do? How do I go about it?"

He smiled. "There's no strict formula. But one thing's for certain. You have to find out who the 'thrower' is. You have to track the *'jettatore.'*"

"You mean *jettatrice.*' I'm positive it's a woman." She offered him anisette out of an old china boar. Pouring, she continued, "It's a bitch, a female witch. I know it."

He inhaled the anisette in his cup, then drank the contents in one swallow. "Okay, I trust your instincts. But Fortunato intrigues me. I have good instincts too, and they tell me he had something to do with this."

Minnie looked pained and wrung her hands. "I'm sure it wasn't him."

"I don't say he's the 'thrower.' But I think he's connected in some way." He clamped the cigar in his teeth, puffing until the ash glowed.

"How is he connected?" Minnie asked.

He shook his head. "That's one of the things we have to find out."

She tightened her grip on his hand. "How do we begin? You must help me."

He patted the gripping hand. "Sure I'll help, Minootch," he said. "I'll help all I can. But *you* are the expert in detective work, and that's what must be done."

Her hand dismissed the notion. "I'm no detective. I just had to protect my son against that killer, Guerra. I finally figured out he was impersonating the priest. It just came to me. I'm no detective."

"It came to you out of the blue? You didn't think about it, try to track down the killer?"

"I wanted no part of it. But I had to protect myself and my son. The mad man killed my husband in Sicily, then he comes here and starts murdering people and putting corks in their mouths the same way. I *had* to do something." Minnie shifted the weight on her plump bottom. "So I found out who he was."

"And killed him."

She winced. Admittedly, some aspects of the adventure had thrilled her. But the shooting had been an entirely ugly experience. "He was about to kill my son on the altar of God. What could I do?"

"Nothing else," he admitted. "Look at it this way, you freed him from his suffering. He was a profoundly unhappy man."

"That's not for me to say."

"In any case, your talents are called for again."

"Again," she said wearily, wrapping the word in a sigh.

"You have to come up with the suspects, think about motives."

"Yes. Examine what happened before the baby died, look for clues."

"You have to steel yourself," he said, cautioning with his index finger. "Remembering won't be easy."

"*Beh,*" she grunted. "It doesn't hurt any more. I just want to get that witch."

"When did the baby first start feeling sick?"

"Right after baptism. After the amulet got lost."

"Wouldn't you say he most likely was 'overlooked' on the very day of the baptism?"

She pondered the possibility. "Anybody could have gotten the chance that day."

"Wouldn't an envious witch pick a ceremony or a feast?" he suggested.

She looked at him with admiration. "You're right. It was done in church."

"Or at the party afterwards."

Minnie looked momentarily defeated. "There were so *many* people around. It could have happened anywhere."
"That's no way to talk. You'll find her."
"I remember the church was crowded." Thick lashes fluttered over her hazel eyes. "It was such a happy day."
"I thought you said it didn't hurt any more," he reminded her.
"It hurts like a headache now, not like a knife."
"But you've been living on the edge?"
She balled her fists. "Why did it happen to Stefano on such a joyous day?"
"Envy was in the air."
"Why?" she repeated with furious insistence.
He smiled tolerantly. "They say why is a crooked letter."
She burned him with her eyes. "Don't joke."
"I'm not joking. Ask what, not why."
"I still say, why us?"
"Your ancestors were sent floods and famines. They suffered earthquakes and epidemics. Excuse me for asking, were you given some special dispensation?"
"I can't be a stoic."
"To be stoical doesn't mean you have no passion. It's just that in the end you accept."
"Not without a fight."
"Not without a fight," he agreed, extinguishing the skinny cigar with his fingertips and putting the butt in his breast pocket. "So let the fight begin."
Minnie still craved a cigarette but ate a biscuit instead. As she reflected, crumbs fell to the plastic tablecloth. "Will I have to kill her?"
Arturo looked at his friend, at the lines of distress etched into her face. Behind her, tacked to the wall, was a framed motto: *"Chi va piano, va sano e va lontano"*—"He who goes slowly, goes soundly and far." "There's no script for it," he answered. "It depends." He squinted. "You must be prepared for anything. Maybe she—or he—will try to kill *you.*

First, let's find out who the witch is. Then we'll know what to do."

She finished the biscuit and patted her lips daintily with a cloth napkin, her eyes lowered. "Where do we start?"

"The Bible calls envy an evil eye," he said." Who envies you?"

"Most people like us."

"Another reason to envy you. The witch is envious either of you or your son, to narrow it down."

She bit her thumbnail. "Or of Cynthia."

He nodded. "That's possible."

Minnie was suddenly inspired. "I think I know who it is."

"I have a hunch myself," Arturo added, raising his forefinger to his lips. "But don't say the name."

"Why not? We have to share information if we want to work together."

"Not yet. To utter a false name now would be unlucky. Let's do a little investigating first."

Minnie hissed, impatience rising as if through a fumarole. "More horns against the evil eye?"

He bottled up his annoyance at her condescending tone. "There are many ways to explain things, eh, Minnie. Some people talk about expanding universes, black holes in space. That's not my language. What's the difference, really, between black holes and black magic? I would say the only difference is language. Let's consider ourselves scientists of the spiritual, you and I. No materialist has ever explained, in a way that satisfies me, why misfortune visits some people more than others. I prefer to call it the evil eye."

Minnie again recalled the conversation with her father about viruses so many years ago. She felt somehow chastened.

"All right, Arturo. We'll do it your way."

He grinned, displaying stained teeth. "I want to make a little investigation. I'll let you know how it comes out."

Minnie Santangelo and the Evil Eye

Minnie swatted a voracious, fat fly off her forearm. "I have an investigation to make too," she told him.

"Fine," he said, with a toothy smile of reassurance. "We'll compare notes."

Within an hour, Minnie's heels resounded on the tiles of Saint Theresa's Church where the scent of incense lingered from a benediction ceremony, blending with the odor of altar flowers. She reached the main altar and genuflected, catching a glimpse of Father Mancuso in the sacristy.

She motioned to an altar boy who, with an air of importance, was extinguishing candles with a brass snuffer. He frowned and made a great show of finishing his task before responding. Raising his cassock to avoid tripping, he descended the steps to the railing and inclined his head. He was chubby, with red cheeks and hair of indigo, a stray lock curling over his alabaster forehead.

"Please tell Father Mancuso that Mrs. Santangelo wants to talk to him," she whispered.

He nodded and entered the sacristy, vestments rustling.

She sat in the first pew, fixing her gaze on a side altar dedicated to the Blessed Mother. The eyes of the statue were raised in plaster supplication. The arms were outstretched, palms outward, fingertips pointing to the bright spikes of gladioli. Folds of her carved veil and vestments were chipped at the edges. Minnie prayed hard to the flawed effigy.

The altar boy reappeared to inform her the priest would receive her inside the sacristy in five minutes. She smiled perfunctorily and he left, gathering up his cassock with the majestic air of a future bishop.

She again gazed at the statue of the Blessed Mother, the maiden understudy of Pallas Athena, Minnie's patron saint. She gazed with fervor, a prayer on her lips, resolution smelting inside her. She said five Hail Marys before getting up off her knees and heading for the sacristy

Father Mancuso appeared at the door with a flurry of welcoming sounds. His morose mouth was bent in a smile as he ushered her to a folding chair pulled up to a Danish-modern desk. He had removed the embroidered chasuble and other vestments and was dressed in a CYO sweat shirt and jeans. He donned an expression of priestly sympathy. "Signora?" he said.

Minnie launched the conversation with no preamble. "Do you remember the day of my grandson's baptism?"

He hunched his shoulders and gestured as he spoke. "Of course I do. But why torture yourself with such details, Signora? Accept God's will, hard as it may seem. . . . "

"I'm not asking to torture myself. I want to know if you remember who was in church on that day. I have my reasons."

"Who attended the baptism ceremony? Practically the whole neighborhood. You know that." He glanced at his watch. "I have to referee a basketball game in five minutes."

"Do you know a girl named Valentina? Valentina Corvo? She used to live in the neighborhood."

"Umberto Marrandino's niece?"

"Yes. Would you recognize her today?"

"Sure."

"Was she in church for the baptism?"

"Everybody was in church that day," he said, making a sweeping circle with his right hand.

"Do you remember seeing her specifically?"

His eyebrows met over the bridge of his hawk nose. "As a matter of fact, yes. She wore black, that's why I remember." He laughed, nervously. "I remember thinking it's supposed to be bad luck to wear black to a baptism."

Minnie rose agitatedly. "Thank you very much, Father."

"Why do you want to know?"

Minnie would not lie to the priest. "I don't want to say just yet. Thank you again, Father, for your help."

He got up from his chair looking bemused. "What is all this?"

She bowed, "Good afternoon, Father."

On the way out, she knelt again before the statue of Mary, focusing on the Virgin's feet which were crushing down on the head of the serpent whose leering mouth seemed smeared with cochineal.

She left the church.

Chapter 19

A yellow moon illumined the stream of traffic down Church Street. Valentina, smoking a cigarette, watched through a corner window. It was nearly midnight and Ray was still asleep.

After a short, energetic bout of sex, he had burrowed into sleep, avid for forgetfulness. He was still snoring deeply.

She sat propped against the rattan headboard, smoking and listening to Brazilian music on the stereo. Her gaze shifted from the traffic to the minute movements of his face, a strong face which in sleep seemed chiseled from sallow marble. His left arm formed an arabesque over his head and his slack, uncircumcised penis curled against his thigh.

She squashed the cigarette and hopped out of bed, heading for the kitchen at the far end of the spacious loft. Tina often had the big place all to herself since Kate Haley, her actress roommate, made frequent road trips. Right now, she was on movie location in Mexico and would be away for at least another month.

The place was attractive and comfortable, if not luxurious,

with lots of plants, brick walls, a skylight, and huge working fireplace. Tina enjoyed living there mostly alone.

She rummaged in the refrigerator and brought out a half bottle of Chablis and a wedge of aromatic provolone. She poured a glass, broke off a piece of cheese, and ate it robustly, washing it down with wine. She brought the remaining cheese and wine back to the bedside.

Ray mumbled and shifted his body as she placed the food on a wicker night table. Then she donned tan pleated shorts and a yellow tee shirt and began brushing her hair, reflecting on the events of the day. For the moment, she had what she had wanted for a long time: Ray Santangelo in her queen-sized bed. The only question was how to keep him there.

Smiling to herself, Tina brushed her raven hair. If Nonnetta were alive, she would know what do do. She remembered a proverb her little grandmother had indocrinated her with as a child: "The man is the bee and the woman is the hive." Nonnetta would have provided a formula for holding on to Ray.

Frowning, she continued to brush. What would Nonnetta have thought of her job as a topless barmaid? Of course, she never would have approved, but she probably would not have condemned either. Self-righteousness was not in her. Tina wished she could be like her grandmother, live according to her rules. Nonnetta died like an angel with a smile on her face. She must have known something.

Tina tied her hair in a pony tail and rummaged for a book in the shelves built around the brick fireplace. She chose a gothic novel, established herself in a basket chair near both the window and the food on the night table and read until dawn. When she finally fell asleep, she saw the confident face of Nonnetta, a prune of smiles.

While she dreamt, Ray woke up. He winced as consciousness flooded back, breaking the spell. He focused his eyes on the green wine bottle which he grabbed by the neck and drank to the dregs. He sat up in bed and saw Tina asleep in the chair by the window. His eyes traced the downy hair on the inside of her thigh. Immediately, he wanted to have sex again, make another bid for forgetfulness.

He got out of bed and woke her up with a hard kiss on the mouth, to which she responded by curling her hands like soft petals over the back of his head. He picked her up from the chair and carried her to the bed.

They melted into one another, legs and tongues interwined, hands moving all over each other's bodies. She held the staff of his penis as he removed her clothing.

An hour later she asked him if he wanted breakfast.

"Do you have any tequila?" he asked, eating a piece of cheese.

She frowned. "Don't kill yourself with alcohol."

"Why not?"

"It's too slow. I'll see what's stashed." She walked back to the kitchen and checked the liquor supply. "Will *grappa* do?" she shouted.

"Sure."

She returned with a tumbler and poured a neat shot. "Smells like poison," she said as her bare breasts swung over the glass.

He smiled. "Still the topless barmaid."

She scowled at him. "Better than an unemployed, alcoholic lawyer."

"Shove it," he said before downing the fiery brandy. He set the glass down. "Leave the bottle right there."

She hesitated, then shrugged and walked over to the old-fashioned armoire where she stored her clothes. She flipped through the hangers, finally selecting a robe of Japanese silk, beige and yellow, trimmed with Oriental calligraphy. She tied the sash and looked at him grimacing at the burning *grappa*.

"Don't like it much, do you?" she said.

"Ambrosia," he answered, looking glum.

She gathered up his soiled clothing from the parquet floor.

"There's a pair of jeans and a blue checked shirt in the armoire that should fit you. The bathroom is to the right of the kitchen. You'll find a toothbrush and a razor."

"Would you like to pick the lice out of my hair too?"

She stopped with his clothing bundled in her arms and looked at him icily. "If you wish."

He avoided her eyes, drank silently.

Tina felt a pang of compunction. He was suffering so, why shouldn't she humor him, indulge his craving for anesthesia? Hadn't she decided in the Lolita Lounge that she would take him on his own terms? Perhaps, after a while, he would allow himself to be coaxed back to a point where he could face things. And she would be there to help him. She dumped his clothes into the hamper and refilled his glass.

Furtively, he watched her go over to the armoire and return with the shirt and jeans. She dropped them on the bed. "Put them on, if you like."

She retrieved the book she had been reading and sat by the window.

Half an hour later, he emerged from the bathroom, showered, shaved, and with the clean clothes on his back. Tina was still sitting by the window, caught up in the novel. She glanced at him and said, "There's cold chicken in the fridge. I also have cheese, pâté, and a nice chilled Verdicchio."

He poured another shot of *grappa* and sat down beside her, looking sulkily out the window. "I *am* a little hungry," he admitted.

There was a hint of triumph in her smile. She slid gracefully out of the chair. "I'll rustle us up something."

She went back to the kitchen, swaying her plump hips. Her body was beautiful, he thought, although on the fleshy side, suiting her *demi monde* way of life. As he recalled she used to be thinner, never wiry like Cynthia, but thinner.

There was a rap at the door, a figure dimly visible through the chicken-wire window pane. Tina called out from the kitchen. "See who it is, will you?"

Drink in hand, Ray walked over and swung open the door. The visitor had hair the color of wheat, a brush mustache, and he wore a black eye patch. "How d'you do."

Ray nodded dourly, looked him up and down. Tweeds, suede boots, pink fingers, class ring.

"Val home?" the man asked, extending his hand. "Name's Hampton."

Ray declined the handshake and stepped aside. "She's in the kitchen." With a shrug of indifference, Nick Hampton walked in.

She carried a tray of food with a vase of flowers on it. Her smile dissolved. "Nick."

Hampton smiled pleasantly. "Brunch, how nice. But you needn't have bothered."

Ray looked at her sharply. "You knew he was coming?"

She fixed her eyes angrily on Hampton. "His idea of a joke. What do you want, Nick?" She placed the tray on an end table.

"The pâté looks good." He sat down in a canvas chair. "Do you have any pumpernickel?"

Scorn twisted her smile. "This isn't the Harvard Club, Nick. Get out of here."

"But it's so cozy."

"Take a walk," she ordered.

A mock pout appeared on his smooth face, the eye patch enhancing the farcial look. "I love you when you talk tough. So sexy, so ethnic."

Ray clenched his teeth. "How would you like a hero sandwich full of knuckles?"

Hampton measured Ray from the chair. "Pungent wit. Please spare me the line about giving me another black eye. I've heard it too often."

Tina noticed that Ray was flushed. "Take it easy," she advised him.

"By the way, Santangelo," Hampton added, "I thought you people wore black armbands."

Tina gripped Ray's arm. "Don't let him reach you. That's what he wants." She faced her husband. "Unless you have a damn good reason for this visit, I suggest you split, Nick. Now."

"My, my, this is a first—a topless bouncer," Hampton said.

"Excuse me," Ray said, picking her hand off his arm, "while I take him apart."

Hampton produced a folded document from his jacket pocket. "Just sign this, Val, and I'll be going."

"What is it?" she asked, walking over to him and examining the piece of paper.

"A legal separation agreement," Hampton said. "I'm sure you'll find it satisfactory."

She looked up from the document and into his face, his gently mocking smile. "Just look this over," he urged her. "That's what the agreement gives you. Exactly nothing."

She took the document from him and looked at it again, cursorily. "Why didn't you have it sent through your lawyer?" she asked.

"You know how sentimental I am," he said.

"I'll read it when I get the chance and mail it back to you."

"Then, can we get together with the lawyers and sign it?"

"Unless it calls for me paying *you* alimony."

"You mean you'd begrudge me?"

"I thought you were leaving."

"Not even a splash of wine to mark the occasion?"

"It's too early to drink."

"That looks like Verdicchio. An inferior wine, but then it was an inferior marriage."

"You said it."

He sighed. "I'll miss your body."

"You know where I work."

"But I can only look at it there."

"That's all you know how to do properly anyhow."

"You might at least have taught me something. Let's reconcile and I'll take lessons."

"Like the tennis lessons when you went to boarding school?"

"I had archery lessons, remember?" He looked at Ray. "That's how I lost my eye." He said to Tina, "In any case, that's my last offer. Surely it's better than hustling your tits every night."

"No, it isn't."

"Really?" He seemed genuinely puzzled.

"You may know your wine but you don't know your women," she said.

"I admit I lack discrimination in that area. I have a palate for saucy women, while I prefer subtle wines."

Ray said, "Maybe you ought to switch."

Nick frowned. "You mean to beer?"

Ray turned to Tina, "Let's show Oscar Wilde to the door."

"Are you impugning my masculinity?" he mocked.

Ray bowed icily. "Merely paying tribute to your wit."

Nick rose from the basket chair. "I suppose I'll have to leave without a libation." *Buona fortuna, Cavaliere,*" he said coldly. "You'll need it."

Ray felt uneasy under the cyclopean stare.

Chapter 20

Minnie removed the wrinkled bedsheets, damp mementos of her sleepless night. Ray had not come home and she spent the hours tossing and fretting. She needed sleep to be strong. Was Tina the witch? Minnie was fairly convinced of it.

Yet she would keep an open mind. Life had schooled her in circumspection, and she must be absolutely certain before taking action. It would be dangerous to single out the wrong person.

With Tina, the pieces of the puzzle all fit, perhaps *too* neatly. She had always been infatuated with Ray. Minnie remembered when Ray was a teenager and took out another girl besides Tina—a girl named Nina, Nina Carbone. Nina and Tina, they were always joking about it. But it was no joke to Tina. Even at fifteen Tina had a frightening capacity for anger, and she threw a glass through Ferrara's window and gave Ray a black eye with her fist.

One spring day, Nina Carbone was run over by a car right on Mulberry in front of Curcio's port store. The fat women who sat on folding chairs, sunning themselves at the tenement doorways, gasped in shock, wrung their hands in sorrow.

Everybody called it a freak accident. An old man had suffered a heart attack at the wheel of his Chrysler and lost control. He lived. There were whispers about Tina Corvo.

Not that anyone thought Tina directly had caused the accident. The man was a lawyer driving home to Forest Hills and had no connection with the neighborhood. And Tina had been nowhere near the scene of the accident.

Still, there were whispers.

Tina and her family had always been the subject of neighborhood rumor. Her father was in jail, her mother not quite right in the head, according to local gossips. And her godfather Umberto, now passed away, was a member of the *onerata società*.

To make matters worse, there were stories about how Tina talked to animals. Besides dogs and cats, she kept a pet snake. This wasn't normal.

Minnie changed the sheets on Ray's bed too, the one that Minnie and her husband bought on Fourteenth Street when they got married. She shook her head as she bundled up the linen. Her marital bed was now her son's bed of nails. He was in such torment.

Minnie was determined not to mention her suspicions about Tina to anybody yet. She had the Italian gift of gab, but she also shared her compatriots' appreciation of the value of silence—*omertà*. How did the saying go?—"*La meglia vendetta e la parola che non se dice*—the best revenge is the unspoken word." She had to be positive about Tina before she said anything.

Ray walked into the apartment, his glum face a shield against guilt. Minnie could not bring herself to add chastisement to his pain, so she disguised her disappointment in him.

"Can I get you coffee, fix you breakfast?" she asked.

"Don't bother."

"How about egg yolk with sugar, like I used to make you?"

"No, nothing. Please don't baby me." He sat down at the kitchen table and loosened his shirt collar. "Don't you have a stash of Marsala somewhere?"

"Who *else* should I baby?"

His face darkened. "Don't mention that word. Don't ever say it," he commanded.

"You said it first." Now Minnie's compassion for her son flowed freely. She sat beside him, while tears washed her plump cheeks. "Oh, Remo, you drink too much, stay out all night, you don't work. Stop before it's too late. Where did your ambition go, your pride? You were going to practice law, help the people of Little Italy to live a dignified life. Do it. As a memorial to your son. I beg you, face your sorrow and go on about your business. It's the only way."

He shook his head vigorously. "I don't care about anything. Not about anything. Where's the wine? Leave me alone."

"You must care." Minnie rose to her feet. "You must. We can't be beaten by this."

"I have nothing *left* to care about."

She concealed the stab of hurt she felt at this remark. "Remember, Remo, no matter what happens, you always have yourself," she said, pointing to her gut for emphasis. "You won't always have me."

Remorse struck Ray like a blow. He burst into tears.

She cradled him in her arms, rocking him, soothing him. "It's all right, *figlio mio,* everything is all right. Things will get better now."

He hid his face from her, rubbed his eyes with his knuckles.

"Don't be embarrassed," she admonished him.

"It seems unmanly to cry."

"It's unmanly only to cry for the wrong reasons."

He smiled for the first time in weeks. "I'd like to get some sleep."

"There are clean sheets on the bed."

Anthony Mancini

* * *

Minnie was watching a television soap opera when Arturo phoned. She was excited to hear his voice. "Where have you been for the last couple of days?" she asked. "I've been trying to reach you."

"I took a little trip," he said conspiratorially. "I'll tell you about it when we meet. How have you been?"

"Not bad. I have a few things to tell you, too. When will we see each other?"

"How about tonight?" he suggested.

"Sure. Come on over."

There was a pause on Arturo's end of the line. "It's best to talk about private things in public places. Let's meet at the coffee house."

"You mean Dante's on Mulberry?"

"They have excellent *sfogliatelle.*"

"Fine." Minnie could not contain her impatience. "Where did you go on this trip?"

"I'll tell you when I see you."

She felt a vague disquietude. "You sound worried. Is anything the matter?"

His laugh had a sad, resigned quality. "I think the wolf is in the garden."

Minnie wrinkled her brow. "In heaven's name, what do you mean?"

There was another pause at Arturo's end.

"Maybe it's nothing, but since yesterday I've had a headache. A very bad headache."

Chapter 21

Minnie was very agitated when she arrived at Dante's coffee house, but despite her fear for Arturo and the sadness of recent events she could not suppress a shiver of pleasure. It was more exciting than the TV soap operas. First she was the goddess Minerva, and now she was Diana on the hunt.

She ordered a double espresso from Dante's son Michael, the kid who had just won money on the Celebrity Sweepstakes show, and sat in a sidewalk-café chair under a Campari umbrella to wait for Arturo.

It was Friday, a warm October evening with Mulberry Street in polyglot song. A husky Italian sold oranges to a frail Chinese housewife, a black plainclothesman expertly forked spaghetti while tourists strolled, clicked their camera shutters, and gawked. Little Italy, decorated in banners of red, white, and green, preened like a Roman adolescent in front of a foreign girl. Minnie found a comfortable position in her chair to watch the scene.

A letter from Cynthia's mother had arrived that afternoon,

increasing Minnie's agitation. When he had emerged rumpled from his nap, Minnie silently handed Ray the letter.

Ray poured a cup of coffee and sat down to read. His grim face telegraphed trouble. His wife had suffered a so-called "nervous breakdown" and was hospitalized in Baton Rouge. Her mother wrote that Cynthia had given "explicit instructions" to tell Ray not to come. Minnie grunted. If they didn't want him to come, why didn't they leave him in ignorance? It had alway been a shaky marriage, Minnie reflected as Michael delivered the double espresso. A fledgling mustache feathered the boy's upper lip.

Ray had become even more depressed, drinking the bitter cup of guilt with his coffee. So Cynthia was gone too. His life was ashes. The letter also contained other disquieting news. Cynthia had given her mother something to send to Ray. He turned the envelope upside down, shook it, and a coral horn fell onto the table.

Now what did this mean? Minnie thought as she dumped sugar into the coffee. Cynthia had removed the amulet, but why was she sending it back now? Was it an act of revulsion? Did she believe, without fully admitting it, that removing the horn had contributed to her own son's death? Or was she trying to punish Ray, to symbolize her estrangement from the Santangelos? Its significance eluded Minnie.

Where was Arturo? Mulberry Street turned sepia in the setting sun, Mulberry Street in the fruit orchard of Little Italy, a place that kept its natural charm under a veneer of self-consciousness. Doctor Bevilaqua came into sight.

He blinked at Minnie through rimless glasses, overcame his shame, and spoke, "Signora, I could not face the funeral. I know it doesn't help, but I'm sorry. I don't know the right words, but any words are better than silence."

She touched his forearm. "It was out of your hands," she said with a look that convinced him she was sincere.

Relief softened his sad, pinched features. "Is there anything I can do to help?" His eyeglasses glittered with sequins of fading sunlight.

Minnie's reply was the eternal shrug.

"A psychiatrist or therapist? He would talk to you free of charge." He blushed slightly. "Not that I think you are not mentally sound, you understand. But sometimes, such people can help."

Minnie smiled to reassure him. "I wouldn't know how to talk to a psychiatrist."

He raised his eyebrows skeptically. "I think you would. But not many psychiatrists would know how to talk to you, I'm afraid. Maybe I'm too harsh on them."

"I'd just feel silly talking to one," she confided.

He smiled and withdrew with a bow, resuming his newspaper reading at a nearby table while Minnie went back to watching the passersby.

As usual, the street teemed with Orientals from Little Italy's expansionist next-door neighbor, Chinatown, and with restaurant-goers in polyester. The unmistakable form of Fortunato Ricci hove into view, a shambling apparition in the descending darkness. Enthusiastically, she waved to him.

He saw her and crossed the street to the coffee house. As he approached the table, Minnie smiled, "*Caro* Fortunato, sit and have coffee with me. Sit, sit."

He showed missing teeth in a facsimile smile. "In the evening, coffee disagrees with me."

"Stay anyhow. I'll buy you a lemonade."

He sat down in the chair opposite her. "*I* will buy the drinks," he insisted, drawing himself up.

"As long as you stay awhile," she said, folding her hands in her lap with a satisfied look.

Fortunato took a cigar from the breast pocket of his shirt. He always wore a white shirt, and his hair slicked back. "You're a good soul," he told Minnie. "You know how to talk to a person."

"I enjoy your company," she protested modestly.

He lit the cigar, squinted at the flaring match, then blew it out. With a baronial air, he ordered espresso and lemonade from the young waiter. His face, skeleton pale, looked glum. "I am very sorry about your grandson. It seems that good people always suffer."

"I have accepted it now. We have to accept, you know."

"I know, but we don't have to like it."

"You can always try to change the things you don't like."

"Yes. If you're able to." He looked forlorn. "I told you I shouldn't have come to the baptism party. I told you."

She shook her head vigorously. "You had nothing to do with it, Fortunato. In my heart, I'm sure of that. Please don't blame yourself."

He puffed slowly on the cigar. "I wish *I* was so sure." He sought her eyes. "Sometimes I think I have committed a crime of honor, an enforced sin that I cannot even confess to a priest. I feel that I am cursed."

"*Sciochezza*," scoffed Minnie. "Plain nonsense."

The boy brought coffee and lemonade and they fell into silence. Fortunato gazed with distaste at the frenetic activity on the street. Finally he turned to Minnie and said quietly, "It was *malocchio*."

She stared intently at the pale face wreathed in cigar smoke. He repeated, "It was the evil eye. I feel certain of it."

She sighed and admitted, "I think so too."

"I was born under a bad eye, that's for sure."

"Not necessarily."

He chuckled in gentle derision. "Just look at me."

"You're smart enough to know it doesn't matter," she chided him. "How you look is in God's plan, and the whole picture is beautiful. To me, it is."

He was gratified by her words but not convinced. "Maybe I am what they call a *jettatore*. Against my will, even, I cast the evil eye."

Minnie Santangelo and the Evil Eye

The street lamps gleamed on Minnie's hand trembling on the cup. "Has anything happened to you in the past to make you believe that you are a *jettatore?*" Minnie asked. "Have you brought misfortune on people before?"

"My whole *life* is a misfortune."

She made a dismissive gesture with her hand. "What foolish talk, Fortunato. I'm surprised at you."

"I believe it," he said, suddenly bringing his fist down on the table. "I believe it with my whole being." He composed himself, smiled sheepishly.

Minnie excitedly pressed her questioning. "Do you remember any times, any specific incidents when you brought bad luck to others?"

He thought the question over. "That's hard to say. I see misfortune all around me and often I think, well, I think that I am to blame."

She was rigid with disagreement. "That happens to everybody. You're no different from anybody else. Tall or short, pretty or plain—pardon my playing the philosopher—we all inherit guilt. That's what you're talking about. But *malocchio?* That's a very special legacy."

She glimpsed the torment behind his cynical façade. "I still believe that I'm cursed with the power," he said.

"That's because you don't like yourself enough."

"I like myself okay," he demurred. "Yes, even my outer self. The stumpy legs and the turtle on my back don't always bother me. You may not believe it, Signora, but there are times when I enjoy the crab's-eye view of life."

"I believe it."

"Other people don't like me much, that's the trouble." He puffed angrily on the cigar. "It's a drag, you know? Except for you. You're different."

"Don't try to get my sympathy," she warned him. "You're too good for that."

A fly eddied, landed on the rim of the coffee cup, seemed to

Anthony Mancini

contemplate the black, brackish pool, then flew away. Fortunato peered at Minnie intently and spoke. "I don't want sympathy. What I say is the simple truth. People avoid me. If I were them, I would avoid me, too." He chortled. "I don't even care all that much."

"What about Sister Anastasia? She cares about you, doesn't she?"

He laughed like a prankster. "She cares about me, but I don't care about her."

Her look was full of rebuke. "Shame on you. She is like your mother."

"Yes," he said, laughing again. "My virgin mother. Purity in black." His mocking laughter died abruptly. "She drinks too much."

Minnie felt sympathy for the nun. "She can't help that. She's such a sad person, and her drinking doesn't bother anybody."

"It bothers me," he said.

If a person is born under the evil eye, Minnie wondered, *does he have the power himself? Does the power become transferred from witch to victim, to others involved?* There was so much she didn't know about this thing.

And where on earth was Arturo?

She fished in her purse for change. "Excuse me," she said to Fortunato. "I was supposed to meet Arturo here, but he hasn't shown up. I want to call him to find out what happened."

She went to a corner pay phone and read the instructions on the box before inserting a dime. In a few minutes, she returned to the table with a worried look on her face. "No answer."

"Maybe he forgot," Fortunato suggested.

"Or maybe he fell asleep," Minnie said. "I'll wait a few minutes longer."

"Another coffee?"

"I've had two and I'm already jittery."

He peered at her. "Is it the coffee making you jittery, or something else?"

She avoided his eyes. "It's the coffee. Too much is no good for you."

"Too bad Sister Anastasia doesn't realize that about the grape." He looked sour.

"The grape?"

"Wine, Signora. She's a hopeless alcoholic."

"She can't help herself, poor soul."

"You're much too compassionate. She can help herself. She's weak, that's all. Weak and disgusting."

"*Dio*, don't talk that way," she admonished, "not about a nun."

"Why not?"

"She's dedicated to God."

He laughed heartily. "The only god she's dedicated to is Bacchus."

Minnie's frown masked a secret appreciation of his wit. "You should speak of her with more respect."

"I *have* no respect for her."

"Don't you at least have pity for her?"

"Very little. Why should I?"

She looked dejected, bowed under the yoke of her own uncertainty about how people should treat each other. To her, love and hate used to be absolutes. She was no longer so sure.

"I don't know," she said. "It's really your business, not mine. But she raised you from a baby, didn't she?"

This time his laughter was almost savage.

"What's so funny?"

"She didn't raise me very high."

Minnie blushed. "You know that's not the way I meant it."

He laughed and laughed, jarringly out of tune.

* * *

Anthony Mancini

Fortunato's bitter laughter echoed in her imagination as she climbed the stairs to Arturo's apartment. She had waited a last half hour at the café. She recalled what he said on the phone about having a headache so she climbed hurriedly, her heart in her mouth.

As she reached the landing, she heard a funny sound coming from Arturo's apartment. A chill ran through her. It was the disgruntled squawk of the cockatoo. Urgently, she knocked on the door. "Arturr'," she called, trilling the 'r' like a trumpet. No response.

She tried the door and it opened. The apartment was as dark and untidy as ever. Quickly she scanned the outer room with its familiar debris of newspapers, books, unwashed coffee cups, and ashtrays brimming with cigar stubs and ashes. He was not asleep on the couch.

With lead in her heart, she edged toward the *malocchio* room. The door stood slightly ajar. Summoning her courage she entered the room, wading into the stale air and the swamp of her fear. The screech of the bird grated on her ears. She looked around.

The mounted heads of wolves and dogs glared at her. The eye sockets of the human skulls were black as plundered graves. She caught her breath when she saw his body lying face down in the corner. The bird flapped its wings.

Minnie froze. Just as she had feared. As she approached the body, she began to sob in rhythmic waves. She squatted and, with a grunt of physical effort, flipped Arturo over and searched his face for life. What she saw next made her catch her breath, grit her teeth, and squeeze her eyes shut. Then she screamed and screamed in chorus with the cockatoo.

It took her about ten minutes to calm down. She collected herself, mustering her determination not to crumble before this new assault. She knew now she faced a barbarous enemy.

Amen, Arturo had told her—accept it—and so she would accept still another lance in the side. She heard his muffled advice: *Fight this evil eye.* She would, Oh *Vergine Maria,* she would. She let go Arturo's cooling hand and rose to her feet.

As she turned to leave the apartment she saw again the hollow eyes of the skulls, blind reflections of Arturo's fate. His own eyes had been gouged out.

Part Four
La Strega

Chapter 22

Minnie withdrew a sum from her small savings account to pay for the funeral of her lonely bachelor friend. She arranged for a one-day, closed coffin wake at Farnese's on Spring Street. The mourners and flowers were sparse.

Dr. Bevilaqua drove them all across the Williamsburg Bridge to the cemetery in Greepoint. The sun glimmered on the surface of the East River and a helicopter clattered above. Ray sat in front with the melancholy doctor, Minnie, Father Mancuso, and Angela in back. The silence was broken by Angela's muffled sobs. Minnie stared soberly ahead as the Fiat came off the exit ramp.

A passing plane cast a vulture shadow over the gravesite as the group arrived for the burial. In a psalmodic falsetto, Father Mancuso said the prayers for the dead. They lowered the coffin into the hole.

Minnie's eyes were dry. On the small concrete headstone was chiseled an epitaph from Dante's *Paradiso:* "*E la sua volontate e nostra pace.*" And his will is our peace. Minnie dammed up the tears. "*E cosi sia, Arturo mio.* So be it."

Angela continued to cry but Minnie's face was set. The witch had caused two deaths in a few weeks—one insidious, the other savage. Once more, Minnie heard the clarion. It was time to confront her. With a vengeance. Her black dress flapped in the scourging wind.

A woman joined the group of mourners just as the service was ending. It was Valentina, dressed in a navy coat and slouch hat. Ray turned with a look of surprise on his haggard face.

"What are you doing here?" he whispered with annoyance.

"Paying my respects." Heedless of her tailored sailor pants, Tina knelt in the damp grass and said a quick prayer at the graveside. Minnie veiled her eyes. Was she telling the truth or was she here to gloat?

Tina rose from her knees and faced Minnie. "My sympathy, Signora, for the loss of your friend."

Looking straight into the young woman's eyes, Minnie held back her head and nodded acknowledgment. Tina's brown eyes wavered. She turned to Ray. "Sorry, Ray."

Her gaze is not as strong as mine, Minnie thought to herself.

Dry leaves floated in the eddying wind. Tina's presence began to soften Ray's mood. "Did you like Arturo?" he asked her.

She stared at swaying branches. "I didn't know him very well. He seemed kind."

"He was a good friend of the family," were the words Ray finally chose. "Like an extra relative."

"He was an unusual man. Are we writing his epitaph?"

"It's written already. By my mother, with a little help from Dante Alighieri."

"Can't we add to it?"

"There's no limit."

"He was a wise old owl."

Ray nodded.

Minnie folded her arms and looked at the girl. "You like to go to religious services? That's nice."

Minnie Santangelo and the Evil Eye

Tina stared at the ground. "I don't go very often."
"You're too modest," Minnie said with a hint of sarcasm, "you were in church not too long ago, too. Don't be ashamed of being religious."
"I haven't been to church in years."
"Oh no?" Minnie tilted her head. Her eyes grew smoky. "Didn't you come to my grandson's baptism?"
Tina's eyes flashed "I wasn't there. I didn't even know about it."
Minnie said nothing, but her eyes said, *you lie.*
Night swooped down and they headed for the cars. They sat in glum silence during the trip to Manhattan. *Why did she come?* Minnie asked herself. *Was she the one?* Ray had gone back with her in her Volkswagen. *Would he be all right?* Minnie was plagued by worry. Tina had lied about coming to the baptism. How could Father Mancuso have been wrong about seeing her? Even if she had been trying to be inconspicuous, Tina was unmistakable. In Minnie's mind, there was no doubt she had lied. But *why?* Minnie mulled it over as the car lurched down Delancy Street.
The Volkswagen glided east under Tina's feathery control. Ray was smoking a cigarette, winding down. She tranquilized him with her strong, quiet devotion. He didn't ask where she was going. She stopped sharply before the bridge. "Let's turn around and drive to the sea."
"What a storybook idea," he said sarcastically. "It's almost November."
"All the better." She quickly checked the traffic and made a wide U-turn. "We could make Montauk in three hours."
"And freeze our butts."
"There's a sleeping bag in the trunk."
"Forget it. Let's just go to your apartment and fuck."
"What's happened to you? You used to savor the preliminaries."
He widened his eyes in mockery. "If there's a lull in the topless business, you ought to audition for the soaps."

She looked through the windshield at the furling ribbon of road. "Maybe I will." She stole a sidelong glance. "I quit my job."

He pretended indifference. "That will disappoint a lot of tit-happy truckers."

"They never got more than a look."

"That's your business."

She winced inwardly but kept a cool front. "Don't give me that. You got Sicilian blood in you." He didn't respond. "Let's go to Jones Beach, at least," she suggested.

He flinched. "You're full of smart ideas. The last time I was there I was with my wife and kid."

"Christ, Ray, I'm sorry."

He softened. "It's not your fault. You wanna go to Montauk, let's go to Montauk."

She gave it the gas.

They rode in silence until they reached the Expressway. After guiding the car into the middle lane, she turned to him. "This time of year, we might even get a motel room overlooking the ocean."

"I don't have the bread."

"I've got lots of cash on me."

"Stuffed in your garter, I'll bet." He immediately regretted it. "Look, I apologize."

She nodded. "I understand. Were you and Arturo close?"

"Not in recent years. But after my father got killed, he was like my *compare.*"

"He wasn't your real godfather?"

"My real godfather died even before my father. Arturo was my son's godfather." His voice grew sour. "Now they're both gone."

"I know, Ray," she said sympathetically. "Too much grief all at once."

"My mother thinks both the baby and Arturo were killed by the same person." As she drove, he watched her face bathed in alternating light and shadow.

She frowned. "The baby wasn't killed, was he? I thought he died of meningitis."

"Yeah, but Mamma thinks the disease was caused by the *malocchio*. The evil eye." He studied her face.

"She believes it literally?"

"Literally. And she thinks the same person who cast a spell on Stefano—the way she put it was, 'fascinated' him—she thinks the same person gouged out Arturo's eyes."

He saw no look of amazement on her ivory face.

"Maybe she's right," Tina said flatly. *"Lu maluocch'."* Her pronunciation was assertively in the dialect.

"Fortunately, she didn't express all this to the police when they questioned her. They would either have locked her up or ignored her completely."

"What did she tell them?"

"Exactly what happened. He failed to show up at the coffee house, she went to investigate and found him that way."

"They believed her story?"

"Why not? It was obviously the truth. Mamma was grief-stricken."

"Do the police have any idea who did it?"

"Not a one. Arturo had a few friends, and fewer enemies."

"Where did this *malocchio* idea originate?"

"With Arturo himself."

Her eyes registered astonishment.

"I didn't get the full story," he continued. "She wasn't all that coherent. What I mean is, she seemed guarded, as if she thought I would think she was touched in the head."

"What *do* you think?" Her eyes were fastened on the road.

He expelled a gust of cigarette smoke. "That she's been having a very rough time of it lately."

"In other words, you think she's touched in the head."

"No. Just susceptible to fancies."

She smiled.

"What's your opinion?" he asked.

The smile was erased. "Same as yours."

By the time they reached Old Westbury, the Expressway traffic was down to a trickle and she picked up speed.

"Let's get off at the next exit and buy a bottle of wine," he suggested.

"I don't think it'll be easy to find a liquor store open around here."

"Let's try."

"I mean it's not like Manhattan, you know. Let's wait until we get out to Montauk. We'll have a nice late seafood dinner, white wine . . ."

"I want a drink now." He put his hand to his forehead. "I feel rotten."

"Drinking won't help, Ray. What's the matter?"

"I don't know. Feel sort of run down. And I've got a really nagging headache."

She turned off the Expressway. "We'll find some booze," she promised. "And the ocean air will cure that headache." She rolled past a stop sign and gunned the motor. "Just you wait and see."

Chapter 23

Minnie was extremely worried about her son. He finally had called to say he would be spending the weekend on Long Island, somewhere near the ocean. He would tell her no more. She knew he was with Tina and, perhaps, in danger.

She pleaded with him to come home but he made fun of her fears. He had been drinking and, with the assurance that he was "a big boy now," hung up on her.

The next morning Minnie decided to take action. She fretted: she had no idea how to play the good-witch role, and she was frightened. Suddenly in the face of her anxiety some words of her father popped into her head, "There is a book on every subject." Immediately, she put on a black sweater and went to the library on East Broadway.

Laden with books like a school girl, she came back by way of Canal Street. The hawkers were out in force, selling from their sidewalk stands a splendid diversity of things—bean sprouts and belts, swordfish and toilet tissue. Determinedly Minnie wended her way through the bazaar.

Anthony Mancini

Driven by her formless fears, oblivious to the honks of the truckers, she crossed the street against the light at Mott, left Chinatown, and entered Little Italy. As she walked down the street, she noticed a blond man with an eyepatch standing in front of a record store. He seemed to be following her progress, but she dismissed the notion and headed for her apartment.

As soon as she got home, Minnie placed the books on the kitchen table and took a notebook and pen from the cupboard drawer. After putting on a kettle of tea, she sat down to her homework.

The first book she picked up was called *Myths and Mysticism in Southern Italy,* by Umberto Fei. She skimmed the thick volume and found a whole section of chapters devoted to *il malocchio*, with detailed descriptions of the history of belief in the Fascination, of rituals, antidotes, and formulas. She licked her thumb and turned the pages.

Dusk burnished the tenements of Little Italy as Minnie read, entirely absorbed, even though she already knew some of the lore from her girlhood, and from what Arturo had taught her. She made notes of two categories: signs by which one can spot a possessor and antidotes to the Fascination. The tools of her trade.

The hours passed quickly while Minnie read, furiously scribbling notes. She went from the first book to a second and a third, scanning certain sections, reading others with intense concentration. Much of what she learned surprised her. She was particularly pleased to discover that the medal of her patron Saint Anthony was considered an effective amulet against the evil eye. In the top drawer of her bedroom dresser was a Saint Anthony medal that had belonged to her late husband. Minnie had given it to him on their fifth wedding anniversary. It had been blessed by the monks of the Cathedral of Padua. She made a mental note to retrieve it as a handy gorgon shield against her Medusan enemy, the envious witch.

She read on. She learned that one is usually born with the

evil eye, that it cannot be acquired unless one is wet-nursed by a bad witch.

She skipped over catalogues of talismans, since Arturo had already briefed her on these and since the deadly game had already passed the point where such petty preventive measures could be of much use.

She came to a section listing the signs by which one may identify the *jettatore* or *jettatrice*, and here she took copious notes: for example, she learned that green eyes might be a sign of the *malocchio*, as might a strange condition called *colomboma*, a keyhole-shaped iris. She discovered that the onset of yawning in a group of people might signal that a witch had been present, and that peacock feathers, also called "Juno's eyes," were considered unlucky since plucking feathers from the goddess's favorite bird would anger her.

Minnie moved on to the antidotes—the various formulas to use in combatting the evil and its possessor. She set her mouth in a firm line and gripped the pen, while casting a sidelong glance at the picture of Christ that hung near the entranceway. Would he forgive her for giving in to the impostures of magic? With no more hesitation, she began the work at hand.

Until the night was inkstain black, Minnie read. She fell asleep at the table with the pen in her hand, to dream of wild boars.

Chapter 24

The next morning a bone-weary Minnie took the subway to Grand Central Station and boarded a train for Norwalk, Connecticut. She chose a car occupied by only two other passengers and sank into the vinyl-covered seat. She searched her handbag for the customary cache of slightly bent cigarettes and, after making sure no one was looking, placed the filter tip in the middle of her mouth and struck a match without a fumble.

Leaning back and puffing, she looked out the window, following the flight of trees in flamboyant fall dress. Her thoughts raced in rhythm with the progress of the train, swirled with the copper leaves blanketing the countryside. Fear stung her to determination. She had to find out for certain whether Tina was the *strega*. She must not misdirect her arrows and leave herself vulnerable. Perhaps this mission to Norwalk would erase the doubt.

When she found Arturo's body, Minnie had discovered he had been to Norwalk the week before. While waiting for the police to arrive, she noticed the ticket stubs on the dresser along with a scrap of paper with a scrawled name and address:

Frank Arrabiata
52 Cypress St.
Norwalk

Next to the name was scribbled a cryptic warning: "Beware the three bridges."

This must have been the trip Arturo had told her about when he called to set up the rendezvous at Dante's. Her son would never believe her, so Minnie had to tackle the job alone. She mused over the phrase, "Beware the three bridges," as the train stopped at Darien, disgorging black women on their daily journey of indenture.

Soon she arrived at Norwalk. The autumn sun burned overhead as she searched for a taxi. The trip was expensive for her modest budget, but there was no other way.

"Taxi, lady?" A wrinkled lemon face appeared at the window.

Minnie meekly nodded and climbed into the back seat. "Fifty-two See-press Street," she said.

The sourpuss driver gave her a jaundiced look. "Sure you got the right town?"

She frowned and handed him the scrap of paper with Arrabiata's name and address. "I want to go there, please."

He scrutinized the hieroglyphic. "*C*ypress Street," he said with scolding emphasis, flipped sun lenses down over his eyeglasses, and started the motor.

As she rode through the center of town, Minnie's heart beat faster. A little guiltily, she savored the excitement of her mission. She was skirting adventure. *Who was Frank Arrabiata? What would he tell her about Tina and the dread evil eye?*

In a short time the car pulled up to an old clapboard house with a screened-in porch on a side street in central Norwalk.

The driver's arm was draped over the back of the front seat. "This is it," he said without looking at her.

She gazed anxiously at the ramshackle place. The front yard was weed-choked and the porch screens pocked with holes. The only sign in this unkempt place that Arrabiata was Italian was the grapevine-arbored driveway.

"Two-fifty," the driver announced defensively. It had been a four minute ride. She swallowed her protests and paid up. He drove away just as she shut the door behind her.

She went up a cement walk to the front entrance where, under a wrought-iron mailbox, was a doorbell. Soon a leathery face appeared behind the screen door, a face that had baked like terra-cotta in the sun. Aqua eyes appraised her.

"*Benvenuta, Seen-yo,*" he said, recognizing her nationality. He swung the door open and made an ushering gesture. "Smell the *basilico?* Enjoy a plate of pasta with me."

His warm nature immediately dispelled her unease. "You eat pasta at 11 o'clock in the morning?"

"I eat pasta sometimes for breakfast, lunch, and dinner. It's been my gasoline for many years."

She laughed and followed him inside.

He was a handsome old bird, a noble aquiline, with a halo of white hair, a rangy body, and an air of health. She judged him to be nearly eighty.

He led the way through cluttered rooms to a kitchen in the rear. She wondered that he had not yet asked her who she was.

Water was boiling urgently in the spaghetti pot so he quickly showed her to a chair and returned to his cooking. Lowering the burner flame, he dumped a sheaf of linguine into the pot. He turned, showed his teeth in a broad grin, and grabbed the neck of a straw-covered wine bottle as if he were roughhousing with a friend. Without asking Minnie, he poured a glass for her and one for himself.

"Wine, too, at this hour," she said with a frown. "Not for me, thank you."

"*Lu vin'e bone,*" he protested in Neapolitan. "They say good wine flows from the fountain of youth." A boastful grin. "Look at me. I drink a glass or two every morning. At least I have since my wife died twenty years ago. Look at me. I'm eighty-three, would you believe it? But I won't force you," he continued, shoving the glass aside. "Mineral water?"

She nodded.

"Are you married, *seen-yo?*" he asked.

She blushed. "I'm a widow."

"You're a good-looking woman."

Her color deepened.

"Don't worry. I'm old enough to be your father. And I go to church." He sat down opposite her, pouring a glass of Fiuggi water. "To tell you the truth, when I was young I didn't believe in the words of priests. But now . . ." He shrugged. "Why take chances?" He swallowed half a glass of wine. "You're new in the parish? I can only give you a dollar this month."

She looked puzzled. "A dollar? A dollar for what?"

"For the missions. You're collecting for the missions, aren't you? I can't give you the full pledge. But I'll make it up next time."

She shook her head. "You're mistaken. I'm not here from the parish."

He looked at her with renewed interest and an edge of suspicion. "So then. What can I do for you, eh?"

"I want to ask you a few questions."

"Who are you?"

"My name is Minerva Santangelo. I came up from New York City."

"Santangelo." He squinted at her. "Are you Napolitana?"

"My husband's family was part Sicilian. I myself am from the Abruzzi."

His eyes lit up and he nodded sagely. "Abruzzese—*forte e gentile.*" A cavalier bow. "A strong and gentle people, that's what they say. Good, then. What's on your mind?"

Minnie Santangelo and the Evil Eye

Minnie hesitated, then plunged on. "A man came to see you last week. His name was Longo, Arturo Longo."

Arrabiata's smile vanished. "Yes," he said curtly.

"What did he ask you? What did you tell him? It is important for me to know."

He rose from his chair. "I must see to the linguine." An uneasy silence followed. He stirred the pasta. "Why do you want to know?"

"It's a long, long story."

He dumped the pasta into a colander to drain the water off. A gypsy moth batted its wings against the window screen above the sink. Arrabiata had a moldering face, like the façades of the *palazzi* on the stagnant waterfront of Naples. "I needed the money so I lied," he admitted. "It was the Depression. Times were hard." He shrugged. "What can they do to me now? It was so long ago."

"Lied about what?" she asked urgently.

He set two places at the kitchen table, pausing to pour himself another glass of wine. His upper lip was stained a burgundy color. "Like I told Signor Longo, I knew they weren't brother and sister but I lied to the authorities anyhow. I needed the money and they needed an immigration sponsor. The family paid me one hundred dollars, a grand sum in those days." He sipped the wine and his smile was a sad, glittering sapphire, transparently blue and beautiful. "Are you a student of history?" he asked Minnie.

"Not much of one."

"I am a Neapolitan," he announced with resignation rather than pride. "And you don't have to be a student of history to know that means I am a thief. I make no bones about it. When the Bourbons lost the throne to the Piedmontese, we Napolitani, as usual, were caught in between. Somebody once said, we were left with only our eyes to weep with. No wonder we steal."

"I don't judge you. I just want information."

"It wasn't a big lie. She *was* my niece, after all. But the baby wasn't her brother. She had no brother. She was an only child and her mother, my sister, died when she was only two, a victim of malaria."

"Who are you talking about?"

"My niece Eva." He looked at her curiously. "What makes you so interested?"

"Eva who?"

"Eva *Niente Nomen*," he said with a twisted smile. "Eva No Name. She was a bastard."

Minnie leaned forward with interest.

He continued, "Her mother shared my name, of course—Arrabiata." He pronounced the harsh name proudly. "But I told all this to Signor Longo. Is he a friend of yours?"

"He was," she said sadly. "He was killed last Thursday."

His shiny brown face registered shock. "Killed for what? By who? What kinda business was this guy in, anyway?"

"He was a good man. He died trying to help me."

"Then what kinda business you in, lady? And why all the questions?" He rose and served the pasta.

"My business is to find somebody."

He hunched his shoulders. "One of those affairs, eh? It's your business. But now you're asking me about my business. Why should I tell you anything?"

Minnie looked forlorn. "It means life or death."

He looked serious, then his smile reappeared. "I'll tell you all I know. For the same reason I told Longo. At my age, you jump at the chance to talk about the past."

"Then tell me whatever you told Arturo. Why did he come to see you in the first place?"

"For information about my niece and the baby."

Minnie was puzzled. What led Arturo to ask questions about this man's niece? She had never heard of Eva Arrabiata or Eva Niente Nomen.

He ate and drank with good appetite while Minnie picked at her food. He broke off a piece of bread, sopped up tomato sauce, and, with a voice garbled with chewing, told his story:

"We came from a village in Campania called Montevecchio, a rotten place. It is on the border of Lucania, that wild region Rome could never tame. Montevecchio was poor, neglected, backward, probably still is. I haven't heard a word about it in over twenty years."

"I've heard of Montevecchio," Minnie said with surprise. "My late husband's mother was born there. When did your niece emigrate?"

"About forty years ago."

"Did she live with you in Norwalk?"

"No. I saw her only a few times. The family arranged for her to live with the unfortunate baby in a Catholic settlement house in New York City."

"So she also had an illegitimate child. It often happens that way—like mother like daughter. I mean no disrespect to your family."

The old man gave her a smile. "It wasn't her child. He was born to the daughter of the rich family. They were ashamed of the baby so they gave him away to Eva and sent them across the sea. A little money travels a long way. *Chi ha soldi, ha amici influenti.* Money makes friends in high places." He drained the glass of wine and smacked his lips in satisfaction.

What did all this have to do with Tina? Minnie wondered. She raised her eyes to Arrabiata's wrinkled face. "What was wrong with the child?"

He had poured another glass of homemade wine and was peering reflectively into it. "He was *un gobbo,* that's all. A dwarf."

Minnie suddenly understood. Arturo's trip to Norwalk was meant to trace Fortunato's background and had nothing to do with Tina. What else did Arturo learn, what information so terrible and revealing that he was horribly mutilated and murdered for possessing it?

Arrabiata stared at her from across the table. "What's the matter? You look like something hit you."

"Something finally did. The truth. The boy's name was Fortunato, wasn't it?"

"Yes," he said, toying with the remainder of his pasta.

"Eva chose the name herself, not for a joke but to show defiance to the world. She was a tough little girl, and something more."

She leaned forward with interest. "Go on. What more?"

He shrugged while his clawlike fingers broke off another piece of bread. "My mother used to say that Eva had certain powers. You know, over animals and events. When Eva was born, my sister Rosina—Eva's mother—was also working for the same people. The rich family had a little girl too, of about the same age as Eva. She's the one who finally gave birth to Fortunato. Anyhow, Rosina wet-nursed both the little girls, so they were like sisters in a way. When my sister died, Eva was sent to live with my mother. I was already in the States. As she grew up, my mother said, she began to exhibit these powers."

"What kind of powers?" Minnie asked excitedly.

"I'll give you an example. My mother was a spinner who was proud of her beautiful silkworms. One day, the little girl gazed on them and they all began to die. To save her livelihood, Mamma sent Eva away. She was old enough then to go to work for the family. There was a traditional relationship between my people and these bourgeois." He snorted derisively. "Bluntly put, it was master and slave. You're not eating," he scolded Minnie.

"I'm not hungry." She took out of her purse the scrap of paper she had found on Arturo's dresser and unfolded it, handing it to Arrabiata. "Do you know what that expression means?"

He glanced at the paper. "Yes, I told Longo about it. It's a variation of an expression my niece would use. 'Watch out for the three bridges,' 'be careful of the three bridges.' She never explained what she meant by it." He waved his hand in exasperation. "She was always half-crazy."

Minnie puzzled over the expression: "Beware the three bridges." Did it mean the Williamsburg, Manhattan, and Brooklyn bridges? She knew intuitively that it was crucial for her to divine the message.

Arrabiata was shaking his head. "I wish I could remember the name of the bourgeois family." He shrugged. "It doesn't matter." He grinned with satisfaction. "Misery finally spares no one in Campania. I heard they fell on hard times and eventually had to emigrate too."

"And Eva? What happened to her?"

"They let her become a nun, in spite of her instability. Are you sure you won't have some wine?"

She let him fill the glass to the top.

On the trip back to the city, Minnie felt a mixture of fear, excitement, and relief. It *wasn't* Tina after all, so at least Remo was safe for now. The news of who her adversary really was startled her at first, then left her burning with the desire for revenge. But she must keep cool, devise a way to apply her powers. Somehow, the idea that she was going to practice magic did not make her feel at all foolish. Her only concern was to win. The train wheels ground to a strident halt at Grand Central.

Minnie was surprised to find Ray at home when she walked in the door of her apartment. He was dressed in jeans and a sweat shirt, sprawled in an armchair in front of the TV set. A half-empty bottle of brandy sat on the side table. Her son looked at her with glazed eyes. "Where you been?"

"On a little trip. I thought you would be gone for the weekend." She smiled. "But I'm happy to see you. Can I fix you something to eat?"

"No thanks. I came back early. Not feeling too good."

She frowned at the bottle. "Brandy is no medicine. What's wrong?"

"Nothing much. Don't bug me about drinking." He got up and switched off the TV set. "Aunt Angela dropped by this afternoon to say hello. Said she'll phone you for a chat. What kind of little trip?"

"It wasn't important." She placed her hand on his forehead. "You're on fire, *figlio mio*, what's wrong?"

He grimaced. "I've got this splitting headache. Came on me a couple of hours ago."

Minnie caught her breath. A headache was a common complaint. It might not mean anything, but she felt like a stone had been dropped in the pit of her stomach. "Why don't you climb into bed," she advised him. "I'll make you some *camomilla.*"

"That's a good idea."

An hour later, under the blinking eye of the city night, Minnie looked in on her sleeping son. His brow was wet with sweat and he mumbled a nocturnal curse. His forehead simmered under her hand, and Minnie frowned in fear.

When her eyes had adjusted to the darkness, she saw a stack of letters on the night table. After a moment's hesitation, she took them back to the kitchen with her. There were five letters, all from Cynthia.

Chapter 25

There was so much to do that Minnie didn't sleep at all that night. As Remo tossed and groaned on the bed, she rummaged through the dresser drawer and found the Saint Anthony medal. She kissed the cold, golden face of her gorgon shield.

Driven by fear and determination, she went into the kitchen to collect the necessary articles for the first ritual: a deep dish, olive oil, and a teaspoon.

Back in the bedroom, she set the dish on a night table near her feverish son and filled it with water from a pitcher. She scrutinized his waxy features and felt certain he had been overlooked. The ceremony would tell the tale.

Trembling slightly, she poured a teaspoonful of olive oil. With the medal in her right hand, she thrice formed the sign of the cross over Remo, each time repeating the Lord's Prayer. Keeping the medal in hand, she repeated this process first over the oil, then over the water.

Minnie's hazel eyes gleamed like burnished copper throughout the ritual. Her cheeks were flushed, her hair straggled in damp ringlets.

She dipped the medal into the teaspoon of oil and let the

soaked charm drip into the water until seven globules fell, forming round rafts on the surface. Calming herself, she waited.

Before long, the seven drops merged into a single, large oval form, an ogling sign. *Fascination.* Just as she had feared. She took another grip on herself, determined not to be intimidated by this new evil visitation. She would have faith in her own powers.

The battle had begun in earnest.

She strode to her son's bedside and crossed his brow seven times with the oiled medal, repeating the Lord's Prayer each time. He stirred, frowned, and mumbled incoherently. There was nothing to do now but wait.

She had considered then decided against calling Doctor Bevilaqua. She knew in her heart he could do nothing for Remo. She saw with burning clarity that her own powers of healing were being put to the test. She prayed she was making the right decision. Two hours passed. Remo's bed was a furnace. The Fascination was very strong. Again Minnie went into action.

In the refrigerator she found a three-sided clove of garlic which she placed in the small cloth bag that had contained her wedding-ring box. She tied the bag of garlic around her son's neck. Again she waited.

Another hour passed wtih no improvement. Minnie noticed to her surprise that as time went by she gained energy. Yet her confidence sagged. Nothing was working. Stronger medicine was called for.

Minnie returned to her reference books and learned something that dismayed her greatly. It was said that if the overlooked person slept after being Fascinated, it would be more difficult to cure him. Remo had recently been escaping into sleep too often, unnaturally. No wonder her job was so hard.

She shut the book, rushed into the bedroom, and shook her son gently, then roughly, trying to awaken him. He groaned, but didn't gain consciousness. After a while, she gave up. She would have to try more antidotes.

Minnie frowned at the distempered walls of the bedroom, then spat on her fingertips. She applied the spittle to her son's purple eyelids.

With an effort, she removed Remo's sweat shirt and returned with it to the kitchen. From the cupboard she produced her largest spaghetti pot, filled it with water, and set it on the stove to boil. In a few minutes, she placed the sweat shirt in the bubbling water to condense away the evil, poking at the garment with a long fork and chanting, "May the Lord heal his suffering and return the curse of the evil eye to the source."

She repeated the chant three more times, swirling the shirt in the boiling water, perspiring from her struggle.

Still another hour passed, but nothing seemed to be working. If anything, Ray's condition was deteriorating. He kept mumbling deliriously. Minnie decided to go on to an even stronger antidote. She collected a salt shaker and kitchen knife and went back into the bedroom.

Now she crossed herself three times, carefully omitting to say *amen*. She made the sign of the cross three times over the dish of water, saying an Our Father, a Hail Mary, and a Gloria. She put a pinch of salt in the water, then doused her index finger with olive oil.

She let three drops fall and quickly picked up the knife. With the knife, she cut through the drops of oil, moving vertically from top to bottom and horizontally from left to right.

She chanted:

>"*Due occhi t'ha toccato,*
>*Tre santi t'ha aiutato:*
>*Padre, Figlio, e Spirito Santo.*
>*Stu malocchio se ne va via*
>*E non piu avanti.*"

Anthony Mancini

"Two eyes have touched you,
Three saints have helped you:
Father, Son, and Holy Ghost.
May this *malocchio* depart
And proceed no farther."

She took the mixture of oil, salt, and water to the kitchen window overlooking Hester Street and Little Italy. She poured the liquid over the rusted fire escape into the street. *"Aqua e sale,"* she chanted. "Water and salt. Whatever the envious witch has invented, let it fail. Let it fail."

She shut the window against the chill October air.

When day broke, Minnie was asleep in a chair near Ray's bedside. Outside, behemoth trucks rumbled down Kenmare Street and old men started their day with cigars and coffee on Mott Street. In the nearby textile houses, black men still baled cotton while nuns made children form lines two by two in the schoolyards. Minnie stirred.

Consciousness rushed in like a flash of light. She got up and looked at Ray. He was lying peacefully but his face was as white as fossil bones. She pressed her ear to his heart. Shallow breathing. His forehead still sizzled. Depression descended but Minnie shook it off. There was work to be done.

She went to market to buy a black pig. She hesitated about leaving Remo alone, but it had to be done. She would make the trip as quickly as possible.

First, she tried the Chinese specialty stores along Canal Street, the ones with a carnage of fish and fowl dressing their windows. But all the pigs they had were already skinned.

Finally, in a store on Bayard Street, she explained her quest to an old shopkeeper with rheumy eyes and a prominent breastbone under an open-collared shirt. He instructed Minnie to return that afternoon with fifty dollars and otherwise to rest assured.

She returned home and looked in on her son. There was no change. She fixed herself a lunch of fried zucchini and chicken livers before making another quick foray, this time to the bank where she withdrew more money from her shrinking nest egg.

Late in the afternoon, she returned to her Chinese connection.

Even though it was a scrawny animal, Minnie had to rest her shopping bag four times on the sidewalk during the short walk home. Then there were the two flights of stairs to scale. Her apartment landing loomed like an alpine summit. As she made the ascent, Minnie thought about Cynthia's letters. She had felt no qualms about reading them. She hadn't understood much of the content, perhaps because of her flawed knowledge of written English. But she was more inclined to believe that it had to do with the letters themselves, confused, rambling essays filled with recrimination and threat. She obviously was not well.

Could the letters have had this ill effect on her son? Minnie did not discount the possibility.

She reached the landing with her burden.

She brought the pig inside, placed it on the kitchen table, and quickly entered the bedroom to check on Remo. He was tossing again, but still unconscious. This thing had held him in its grip for almost twenty-four hours. She felt nibbles of doubt. Shouldn't she call the doctor? Her son's life might be at stake. Yet her instincts told her to stand firm. She recalled Arturo's words, "You're special, Minnie. You can't escape it." She frowned at the figure of her son writhing in anguish.

Wasting no time, she went to the kitchen and hauled down the largest roasting pan she could find from the top shelf of the cupbord. She greased it thickly with lard. The glossy pig fit inside the pan with room to spare.

From the sideboard, she took a full bottle of cheap Spanish brandy, warmed it in a saucepan, and doused the dead animal until the last drop trickled out. She placed the roasting pan on the tiles of the floor.

She fetched the plaster statue of Saint Anthony from the sideboard and placed it on the kitchen table. Next, she surrounded the replica of her patron with two vases of carnations and lit a candle. She placed it flaring on the makeshift altar. The benign eyes of the tonsured saint fell on the effigy.

Minnie worked quickly, mindful of her feverish son. She struck another wooden match, shielded it, and approached the pig. She was reminded of a happier time, when she had served *porchetta* at Stefano's baptism. She knew the monks of the order of Saint Anthony kept herds of consecrated pigs. It was profane to kill or steal them. But black pigs were consecrated to the Devil. She set the pig alight.

It blazed at the feet of the saint.

Minnie invoked the chimeric deities of the *Mezzogiorno:* "O Sant'Antonio, and all the holy souls of the woods, mountains, and the sea, burn with this Devil pig the lice of evil. May they flee in smoke before your benign gaze. *Scaccia 'stu malocchio, Sant'Antonio.*"

Under arbors of garlic and a calendar from the parish church, a large fire crackled in Minnie Santangelo's kitchen while the eyeless pig glared behind the flames.

Chapter 26

As the black hawk of night swooped down on Little Italy, a storm crackled and fulminated in the streets and alleys, lending a fabulous atmoshpere to the familiar place. Minnie stood by the window, keeping vigil by her son's bedside in silent awe of the pyrotechnics.

For the first time in twenty-four hours he spoke, "I'm dry."

Minnie's smile was bright as Calabrian sunshine. *"Figlio mio,* you're back," she exulted. "I'll make you some fresh lemonade."

"I don't feel very well."

"Naturally, you were terribly sick. But you're better now?" Doubt flickered over her face.

"I don't know. I had frightening dreams, and I get this funny feeling."

Her heart sank. "What funny feeling?"

"This feeling that the dreams are not over yet."

Minnie decided not to shield him. She spoke definitively, feeling bolstered by natural confidence in her newfound role. "They were not dreams and . . . maybe they are not over."

He wet his lips in thirst. "Lemonade would be good. What do you mean, not dreams?"

"You have been fascinated," she announced bluntly. "Someone put the evil eye on you."

"If I didn't feel so sick I'd laugh."

"I'll get you the lemonade." She turned to go to the kitchen.

"Did you call the doctor?"

She hesitated, turning around. "He could not have helped."

"Did you ask?"

"No."

"I can't believe this."

"Remo, we must handle it ourselves."

"Too bad we don't have a doctor in the family." He gave up. "What do I care? All I know is, I feel like shit."

She got down the electric juicer Ray had bought her two Mother's Days ago and began cutting the lemons. She said a silent prayer that the bewitchment was off for good. Minnie now believed in the power, lock, stock, and barrel. When she made an act of faith, she stuck to it. If the evil was off, then her job had been successfully performed. Most of all, Remo would be out of danger. Unless the witch did it again. Minnie decided she would have to confront her sooner or later or they would have no rest. She dropped a few chunks of ice into the lemonade pitcher.

She held the glass to his lips. He sipped slowly, then asked, "Who's supposed to have given me the evil eye?"

"Have you passed the convent lately?"

"Practically every day. It's on my way to the newsstand. Why?"

"She has a view of the street from her window. She could have overlooked you from there."

"Who in hell are you talking about?"

"She isn't in hell yet, but she belongs there."

Under his pallor, Ray looked thoroughly exasperated. He repeated, "Who?"

"A witch in nun's clothing, that's who. Sister Anastasia."

He rolled his eyes. "Maybe I'm still dreaming."

"Drink some more," she offered, cupping his chin. "I'll make you soup."

"I can't eat a thing." His voice seemed to be growing weaker.

"You have to try."

He smiled feebly. "Is soup an antidote to the evil eye?"

"No, but love is," she said levelly. *"Fammi stu piacere,* son. Do me a favor."

"You know I will."

She smiled radiantly and hurried off to make the soup. She would make a quick minestrone out of the liquid stock she saved. The vegetables should be fresh and crisp. More antidotes.

As she was preparing the soup, there was a shout at the front door, "Weh, Minootch. Come on an'gimme a hand."

Minnie walked briskly to the vestibule. There in the doorway was Aunt Angela, fat and flustered under a burden of two shopping bags, and a welcome sight. "Angelin'," Minnie greeted her effusively. "What'd you bring?"

"Food, of course. Now what's wrong with you people?"

Minnie toted one of the shopping bags. "Food, What for? Come on in."

"Cause I'm staying a couple'a days. What's wrong?"

"What do you mean?"

"Listen, I'm no dope. You, I haven't heard from in weeks. I come here yesterday and you're missing and Ray, I could see he was sick. Something's going on. You need my help so I'm staying a couple'a days."

Minnie's face grew serious. "You can't help. This is something I have to handle myself."

Each woman placed her burden on the kitchen table. "So

something *is* wrong," Angela said, triumph and concern in her voice.

"But it's something you can do nothing about," Minnie responded dejectedly. "Thanks anyway."

Angela's small, pretty features melted from a frown into a smile of sympathy. "Okay, so you don't wanna tell me. Don't. But I'll stay anyway. I'll cook for you, I'll help take care of Remo, and you can do what you have to do."

Minnie looked pleased. "Okay," she said, rejecting her hesitance. "I'll take you up on it."

Angela sat down heavily. "How's the kid?"

"Better, I think."

"That's good. What did Bevilaqua say was wrong?"

"I didn't call him."

Her dimply face registered shock. "You got another doctor?"

"I didn't call any doctor."

Angela thought she understood. "I'd of lent you the money. Minnie, why didn't you ask me?"

"Don't be silly, there's always money for the doctor. And Bevilaqua would do it for free."

"So . . . ?"

"No doctor can help Remo." She hesitated, then blurted it out, "He's got the *malocchio* on him."

Angela's eyes looked like rolling dice. "Please, not again. Arturo was a good soul, but he put funny ideas in your head."

"Oh yeah. You know the way *he* died."

"Sure. But that was no evil spell. Somebody put his eyes out. A horrible thing, poor man."

"Why was it done to him?"

"Who knows? But you read about crazy things like this every day in the *News*. This time, it was Arturo. New York is like an open crazy house, you know that. But the evil eye? Get outta here."

"If you only knew the things I know."

Minnie Santangelo and the Evil Eye

"What I know is you've been through a lot lately. I understand if you get crazy ideas, Minootch. But I gotta help bring you to your senses. What are relatives for?"
    A low moan came from the bedroom. Minnie and Angela looked at each other, then hurried to his side. Minnie tried to talk to him, "Remo, don't get sick again. Look, Aunt Angela is here."
    He muttered something, made struggling motions on the bed.
    Minnie faced Angela's disapproving look. "Minnie, call the doctor."
    She headed for the phone.

    Agosto Bevilaqua's angular face froze into severity. "Your son probably has pneumonia and some other things wrong with him. I can't tell by my examination alone. We've got to get him to the hospital."
    "Can't you tell me anything more?" Minnie asked.
    "I'm just a doctor, not a magician. I don't know."
    Minnie looked grimly at Angela who sat on the couch, quietly knitting. "I told you."
    The doctor turned his weary face squarely on Minnie. "Told her what?"
    Angela spilled the beans. "She thinks it's the evil eye."
    He continued to look sternly at Minnie. "Seriously?"
    "You bet," Angela affirmed, unraveling green yarn.
    Bevilaqua looked mortally disappointed. "Signora Santangelo," he drawled, his voice mingling sympathy and disapproval. "I know how you feel lately, but this is foolishness. Take my word for it."
    "I know what I'm doing," Minnie said stubbornly. "You got a better diagnosis?"
    "I have no diagnosis, really, but . . ."
    "Like they say, then, I'm one up on you."

He shook his head. "Signora, this is serious. First your grandson, now your son. I can't take chances this time. Who knows what it is?"

Minnie folded her arms defiantly.

"And let me tell you something," he continued. "I know my medicine, too. I used to be a medical investigator for the city, you know. I may not talk like it, but *belle parole* . . ." he waved his hand, "what do fancy words mean? But even a guy like me gets stumped. You remember when they caught that disease at the American Legion convention in Philadelphia? Even Jonas Salk was stumped. Ray's got to go to the hospital."

"I thought the baby died of meningitis. I thought it was certain."

"What's certain? It was the most probable diagnosis. A pretty sure thing, but certain?" He shrugged.

"So I'll stick to my guns."

The doctor was exasperated. "Okay, say it is *malocchio*. would it hurt to send him to the hospital?"

Minnie shook her head firmly. "I don't wanna let him out of my sight," she insisted. "What if the nurse is the witch?"

He searched the heavens for fortutide. "You know what doctors call that, Signora?"

Minnie looked straight ahead.

"They call it paranoia," Bevilaqua said.

"I know what that word means. My father taught me. I still think the witch did it. I'm not taking chances. I know who the witch is. She could get into the hospital."

"Okay," Bevilaqua said challengingly, "Tell *me* who she is, I'll have her banned."

"You can't do that. I have no legal proof."

"So what, I'll have it done anyway. Try me."

"I can't tell you," Minnie said, faltering in her resolution. "Don't ask me how I know it, but these things are not done this way."

Minnie Santangelo and the Evil Eye

The doctor gave up arguing. "I'll give you one day," he announced to Minnie, picking up his medical bag.

"What do you mean?" asked Minnie.

"If he doesn't improve by tomorrow, I'm putting him in the hospital whether you like it or not."

"Can you do that legally?"

"I can find the legal means to do it, if I tell some lies. Believe me, I often feel that my Hippocratic oath requires me to lie when I treat Italians. Why didn't I start a nice practice in Riverdale?"

"Because you couldn't stand living there," Angela said, putting in her two cents, without raising her eyes from the knitting.

"Look, I'll make a deal with you," Bevilaqua suggested. He turned to Angela. "You were going to stay over and take care of these people for a couple of days, right, Signora?"

"That's what I came for," Angela said.

"What if Aunt Angela stays with Ray in the hospital, like a nurse? Then would you let him go?"

"Could you arrange that?"

"Just leave it to me."

Minnie looked at her late husband's cousin. "Would you be willing?" she asked Angela.

"That's what I came for," the aunt repeated.

Minnie hesitated a moment more. "Okay, it's a deal," she finally said, sighing.

"Let's get him ready," the doctor said.

Within two hours, Ray was admitted to Beckman Downtown, another hospital, besides Saint Vincent's, where Bevilaqua had connections. Almost immediately, hospital attendants wheeled Remo to the diagnostic unit for tests, while Minnie and Angela waited in an empty semi-private room. It had been arranged for Angela and Minnie to take shifts by

Ray's bed on a twenty-four-hour basis. If another patient was admitted to the room and complained about the vigils, they would make other plans. But they felt certain no one would complain.

After Ray fell asleep, resting more easily under sedation, Minnie left the hospital. It was just after midnight, but she didn't head for home. There was no time to waste. Since the antidotes hadn't worked, the only thing left was to beard the witch in her den, beg her, cajole her, fight her, do anything possible to make her take back the curse. That's what the books said, and that's what Minnie intended to do. She walked against a stiff wind down Grand Street.

Minnie decided she would kill her, if that's what it took. She hoped it wouldn't be necessary, even though the bitch had murdered her grandson and probably gouged out her best friend's eyes. Minnie didn't want to have to dirty her hands. But she would do it.

Minnie looked down Mulberry Street and faced her place of siege. The crucifix reared like a sentry over the brick Church of Christ's Passion. The convent was at the rear.

Minnie walked toward the place proudly, authoritatively—Athena in a flowing robe, Maria about to squash the serpent's head. So walked Minnie the healer, as if toward the white-washed village of her birth, In the vision that now came to her, she stood on a bluff in Abruzzi under the cobalt sky. The village was on one side of her, the sparkling sea on the other. The sun plunged into the deep while net-hauling fishermen cast stretched-out shadows on the sands. Swallows hovered above the olive trees on the terraced hillside and the scent of jasmine distracted from the miasma of malediction in the air.

She turned her back on the azure goddess-sea and walked toward the bleached village, answering the olden call.

Chapter 27

The changeling mother was preparing for bed. She had removed the stifling habit and donned an uncomfortable flannel nightgown. She rinsed her teeth with plain soap and water and ran her brittle hands through tufty gray hair.

She skipped her Hail Marys and took a drink of Amaretto. After climbing between the sheets she as usual washed her face in her tears.

Sister Anastasia was a dry old woman, but her eyes were fountains, her evil eyes. The eyes belonged to Eva Niente Nomen whose mother belonged to the Arrabiata family, and the Arrabiatas were prone to cry. She cried for the gargoyle child who hated her. Was her love Fortunato's prison, cherished for its familiarity? She smiled to herself. Her ugly butterfly would never fly away from her.

She left the bottle of Amaretto on the night table and closed the eyes of *maleficia*.

Minnie crossed Canal Street and started up Mulberry. She passed restaurant windows framing still lifes of fruit and pastry, collages of newspaper food columns, and entered the church courtyard. The convent, also of brick, was a small separate building. Its front door faced the side door of a corner Chinese restaurant. Firmly, she pressed the doorbell.

The nun opened her eyes.

Minnie tapped her foot impatiently. She refused to consider fear. The Saint Anthony medal nestled in the cleavage of her breasts as she waited. She had just seen the man with the eyepatch on the street again. It was a sign, she thought, as she rang again. But an omen of whose death?

The nun slipped out of bed, cursing quietly. The housekeeper had gone home and the other six nuns in the community had been sound asleep for hours. She went to the closet for a robe, put it on with a querulous grunt. There were never visitors at this hour. Had someone once more mistaken the convent for the rectory? She descended the carpeted stairs, a specter in the half-light. Gold and green panes of glass shone above the front door.

At first Minnie didn't recognize the face, framed as it was by sheared wooly hair instead of the usual white headdress. But as soon as recognition dawned, she launched her assault. *"Monaca maledetta*—you hellish nun!"

The woman stood impassive in the doorway. "We'll talk in the parlor," she informed Minnie.

Minnie's heart pumped as she followed the nun through the convent rooms, lifeless chambers where everything looked like it belonged in a wax museum. The nun sat gingerly on the edge of a Victorian couch. Minnie remained on her feet, balling her fists in anger. "Let me see your eyes," she demanded.

The nun's frown was chipped out of granite, like her stone heart. "Gaze all you wish."

Minnie bridled at this. "I don't fear your glance. My eyes are strong too."

Defiantly, she brought her face up close and looked the nun squarely in the eye. "Your iris is shaped like a keyhole, you witch. You are a *jettatrice.*"

Minnie Santangelo and the Evil Eye

The nun glared icily. Then she nodded. "My middle name is Lucia," she said slowly. "Like the Saint of Syracuse, I shed bloody tears."

Minnie felt like her insides were the bowels of a volcano. "You drench others in blood," she growled.

The nun regarded the woman's fury impassively. "No," she said finally.

"You have the stomach to deny it?" Minnie asked with fierce incredulity.

"I admit I had the power. How did you find out?"

"I talked to Frank Arrabiata. Why do you want to destroy my family? We treated you with respect. What harm did we ever cause you?"

"I never killed with my power. I am not the person you're looking for."

Minnie's certainty was shaken but she soon recovered it. "Do you lie only when your habit is off?"

The nun spoke in a calm voice. "I'm not lying. I have no reason to hate you and I didn't fascinate your grandson."

"Or kill Arturo, or put the *malocchio* on my son? I don't believe you. I don't believe you."

"I burned out my power long ago in Italy," she said quietly. "My eyes are vacant now. I took my prize and ran away." She snorted sardonically. "He was despised by everyone but me, and now he despises me."

Minnie's uncertaintly grew and with it fear. "You were the serving girl with the evil eye?"

"I was," she conceded with a shrug. "Like my mother before me, I am a servant, a whore, and a witch."

Minnie smirked. "All that, and a nun too."

"And a mother," the woman added proudly.

"Not a virgin mother," Minnie said contemptuously, but her hard-won coolness was melting.

"No."

"You slept with the soldier husband."

189

"Twice. He was the only man I ever wanted, don't ask me why. He's just a blur in memory now. But how I hated her . . ."

"You put the evil eye on her when she was pregnant."

"I damned her with praise and burned her with my flaming eyes. Now there is nothing but ashes. So what? I killed nobody, I took the child and she deserved what happened to her. She's a far worse witch than me."

"Who?"

"Fortunato's real mother of course. Her power is stronger, more malevolent than mine, even though we derived it from the same source."

"What do you mean?"

"We both inherited the power from *my* mother who wet-nursed us. She was my rival from the day she was born." She closed her right hand and wrinkles like knotholes appeared on her knuckles. "And she was not as pretty as she looked."

His crooked form came out of the darkness. "So you are my mother," he accused the nun.

Minnie was stupefied.

For the first time, fright haunted Sister Anastasia's eyes. "Fortunato."

"You are the mother of my deformity." He moved closer.

"I don't consider you deformed," the nun said, cowering slightly. "Fortunato, what are you doing here?"

He jerked his head in Minnie's direction. "I saw her come in." He advanced toward her, casting tall shadows. "I wanted to know why she was here. I always knew I had a good reason to hate you. Now I know what that reason is."

The nun tugged at her cropped hair, dropped her disconsolate gaze to her knees. "Your natural mother screamed when she first saw you."

"I hate her too, even though she has no face."

"Then she never looked upon you again. At least, not to your mutual knowledge." The nun grinned. "The family told her you were dead."

Minnie Santangelo and the Evil Eye

"Who is the bitch?" Fortunato demanded.

Sister Anastasia went on, "They gave you to me like another ugly hand-me-down. But, to me, you were fine silk."

"You're a maggot," he screamed.

The nun froze.

"I might have lived gallantly," he cried. "Who is this one who bore me for nine months?"

Minnie broke in, "If you are not the *jettatrice,* who *did* cast the evil eye on my family?"

Sister Anastasia raised her rugged face to smile at them. "You're both looking for the same person."

Fortunato and Minnie exchanged glances.

"After the war, the rich family found it necessary to emigrate too," the nun continued. "They lost their land to an anti-Fascist. In those days, nearly everybody from the other side settled in this neighborhood. So did they."

"Who?" Minnie yelled, reddening. She was suddenly seized by a blinding headache.

The nun faced Minnie squarely. "You should know, Signora, she's *your* relative."

Minnie was dumbfounded.

"That's right," the nun said smugly. "She always harbored envy for you. A relative of your husband on his mother's side. The Neapolitan side. They came from Montevecchio, remember?"

"Jesus, protect me," Minnie implored suddenly.

"Guardarsi Treponti," invoked the nun. "Beware three bridges."

Angela Treponti.

Angela Threebridges.

Aunt Angela.

Jettatrice.

Eyes.

Chapter 28

A Saint Christopher medal dangled over the topless barmaid's windshield as she drove through the desolate streets of lower Manhattan. It swayed before her distraught, ivory-white face. Tina had been searching everywhere for Minnie.

She cruised down the Bowery in the direction of Canal Street, on the outskirts of Chinatown. She was headed for the social clubs and restaurants of Little Italy to ask around for Ray's mother. Tina knew Minnie was in some kind of trouble.

She had caught the first whiff of it when she couldn't reach either Ray or Minnie by telephone this weekend. She had decided to call him after taming her anger at his abrupt ending of their Montauk idyll. She did not believe he was sick, thought he just wanted to go off on a binge. But after she had returned to the loft and gotten a good night's sleep, doubts began to assail her: maybe he really *was* sick.

So she called twice on Saturday night and got no answer. Her first reaction was a new rumble of anger: so he *had* gone on a bender. Where was Minnie, though? Probably at bingo.

Tina went back to sleep, cursing her lover with all the hostility she used to feel at her nightly prayers.

As she drank her morning coffee under streaming shafts of sunlight from the corner window she felt refreshed. Then suddenly, her fears surfaced again. She threw on a Loden coat and drove to South Ferry to do some thinking. Boats bobbed lustily under a windswept sky as Tina stood on the riverside walkway, watching the whitecaps that scalloped the icy Narrows. Something was terribly wrong.

She searched Battery Park for a pay phone. Gulls serenaded a pair of Puerto Rican lovers, their cheeks emblazoned by the cold. She dropped a dime into the phone she had found by the Statue of Liberty ticket windows. She watched squat vessels churn the waters as the phone buzzed over and over in her ears. Her eyes looked hard over the sparkling bay.

She hurried back to the car and drove home, spending the rest of the day in the loft, phoning people who might know where Ray or Minne were. She had no luck until she reached Bevilaqua at his apartment in a renovated brownstone on Sullivan Street. He told her everything.

Tina held her breath at the news of Ray's mysterious illness. She didn't share Bevilaqua's skepticism at Minnie's diagnosis. She clamped her jaw shut. *Malocchio*! Minnie has been dueling with a *strega*.

Her voice was an icicle. "And what's your diagnosis, Doctor?"

A grunt came over the phone. "Can't say, exactly. Encephalitis, maybe."

"What's his condition?"

"The fever hasn't broken, but it's not climbing either."

"What's being done for him?"

"Sedatives and tests. We can't do anything more till we get the lab results."

"He might be dead by then."

"We have no reason to think so. His vital signs are weak but stable. He's a strong young man."

"How do you know he isn't under a spell?"

He snorted in irritation. "How do I know? I don't know whether he was poisoned, plagued, or bewitched. I don't *know* anything. Maybe you can tell me something. I understand you went to Montauk with him on Friday night."

She was momentarily flustered. "That's right," she finally said. "He seemed okay at first. In fact, he seemed relaxed for the first time since the kid died. Then, on Friday evening, he said he felt sick."

"Did he describe the symptoms?"

"A headache. Vague pains."

"Did he say it was a powerful headache?"

"He didn't say."

"Maybe you're the witch."

"It's no joking matter. I love Ray."

"Isn't love a form of bewitchment?"

"I wouldn't harm him. I couldn't."

"Maybe not intentionally."

"No way. I just couldn't harm him."

Bevilaqua cradled the phone with his chin and shoulder and lit a cigar. "I agree with you. I think it's encephalitis."

Tina shelved her doubts. "Where's Minnie now?" she asked.

Bevilaqua shrugged. "Last I knew she was at the hospital. She and Aunt Angela are taking turns keeping vigil around the clock."

"No wonder I couldn't reach Angela," Tina said. She added, "Can I see him?"

The doctor's wiry body was slack and comfortable in a doughy leather armchair. He puffed calmly on the cigar. "It would do neither of you any good. He's unconscious most of the time. He has lucid intervals, but he's under heavy sedation."

"Can I call the room and talk to Minnie?"

He lay the cigar in a ceramic ashtray he had bought near Salerno. "Hold on a moment. I'll dig up the direct number."

Anthony Mancini

* * *

The Saint Christopher medal spun as she turned west, shuffling the sight of the diamond exchanges studding the Bowery–Canal Street intersection. Bitter cold thinned the ranks of pedestrians and restaurant goers.

Tina's call to the hospital had reached Aunt Angela who told her she had no idea where Minnie was, if not at home. Something stirred Tina's suspicion. Angela had sounded unseasonably chilly, giving Tina a funny feeling that the old girl was up to something. Minnie was up to something, too. Tina was sure of it.

She drove toward the Church of Christ's Passion. Would Minnie too bleed like a sacrificial lamb? Not if Tina could help it. What a great *nonetta* Minnie would make for her children. She parked the car in front of the brick church.

Her high heels clattered on the flagstones like old Sicilian castanets. They stopped short.

Minnie's body lay under a hedge at the feet of a marble Jesus. Tina fell to her nyloned knees to succour the healer. She cradled the plump woman in her strong arms and massaged her cheek. "Signora, Signora. Take strength," Tina whispered with soft urgency. "I'm here to help."

Minnie crawled to the surface of consciousness. After the blinding blow of the witch's headache, her first thought was of her son. "I must get to the hospital," she said hoarsely.

Tina frowned, shook her head indulgently. "Ray is being cared for. There's nothing you can do."

Minnie shuddered. "You don't understand. *Il Malocchio.*"

"I do understand. I said I'm here to help." Tina shook Minnie. No use, she had slipped back into unconsciousness. The young woman rose to her feet and looked around. The windows of the church and convent were black. She tensed her muscles and pulled Minnie up by the armpits to her feet, then alternately dragged and walked her to the waiting car. The older woman sleep-walked, drifting in time between the glaring gardens of her childhood and her present desperate work.

She walked, stumbled, was dragged mumbling in pain and fear, until she was finally seated in the car.

Somehow, Tina managed to get Minnie into the freight elevator and up to the loft.

Minnie gradually began regaining her faculties. When they were in the elevator, she had no idea where she was, but she remembered that she was with Tina. At the door to the loft, she recaptured her voice.

"Angela is the *strega*," she announced, propping her back against the wall.

Doubt flashed in Tina's eyes, but Minnie held her gaze, as she had on that day at the cemetery, and Tina's skepticism vanished. *Aunt Angela. It made sense.* "Let's go inside and figure this thing out," she suggested urgently.

Minnie furrowed her brow. "No time."

"We'll act fast, don't worry. These things take planning, you know that."

She gave in, as Tina turned the key in the lock.

Impatience pumped Minnie's pulse with blood, fueled her intentions. There was no time to analyze, to discuss and dissect. But maybe a moment's planning would be wise.

With her hand on the knob and her back to the door, Tina stopped to catch her breath. She said, "Signora, I want to save your son as much as you do."

"Almost as much. You're not his mother."

Tina cracked a smile. "Okay. Almost as much. What's the difference? Let's save him together."

"That's okay with me."

Tina put her shoulder to the heavy door and pushed. They entered the shadowed vestibule, partially illumined by a shaded lamp in the kitchen. She removed Minnie's coat and draped it over an old hatrack. "Are you all right?" she asked the older woman. "Can you follow me into the studio?"

After a visible effort to master her weariness, Minnie nodded. "Lead the way. I could use a glass of wine."

Tina felt a surge of excitement, like a priestess entering the sanctuaries of Paestum, like Persephone beckoning to the Argonauts, sailing into the inky depths of southern Italy. Her alabaster brow glowed, incandescent with sweat. She led Minnie into the outer studio.

Track lights beamed on a brown corduroy couch. Tina did not remember having left the lights on. What she saw next froze her with fear. He was sitting there with a pistol in his lap and a jagged smile on his face. The unpatched eye gleamed in cruel satisfaction.

Chapter 29

He had been smoking the coarse Turkish cigarettes since his fourteenth birthday when his mother gave him a carton of *Tros* and a word of maternal wisdom: "You're going to smoke something, so you may as well smoke the vilest," she remarked, lifting the prow of her aristocratic nose.

From first puff Nick Hampton found them palatable. He now took the latest in the chain of smokes from the unchanged sky-blue package bearing an illustration of the Trojan horse, planted the filter tip between his lips and gestured with the Colt .45. The women sat on a nearby divan.

He lit the cigarette. "I've been waiting for you, Val." A flash of annoyance at Minnie. "I expected you to be alone."

Tina's initial shock now turned to flint. "You half-blind bastard, get your ass out of my place."

He yawned, covering his mouth with the gun.

Emboldened, Tina hissed at him. "By what right do you . . . ?"

He waved the pistol in warning. He looked at Minnie, eyes

narrowing. "Why did you have to bring Mamma Leone along?"

Tina raged in silence—she knew he was crazy enough to do anything.

Minnie stood her ground under the blaring headache and the gun. It was the man with the eyepatch she had seen on the street, the omen. What was his connection to Tina? "Who is this one-eyed rat?" she demanded.

"My husband," was Tina's sullen reply.

"Okay." Minnie took the news in stride. "Why does he hold a gun on us?"

"I don't know," Tina said. "You'll have to ask him."

Nick savored the cigarette and the situation. But then he frowned. The old woman could ruin everything.

Minnie turned to Tina. "I didn't know you were still married."

"Just barely. We're legally separated and have divorce papers on file." Tina talked through her teeth. "Don't ask how I made such a colossal mistake in the first place."

Nick smiled coldly. He'd cut the Dago bitch loose only when *he* was good and ready. He had wanted Tina the first time he'd seen her on Richard Stella's terrace. He liked the way her eyes shone, the way her body shimmered in the blue lamé dress.

The party was at its height. He looked around with a satisfied smile. Richard had been right: it was just what he needed.

He fixed himself a drink and scanned the talent. Richard might be a trendy photographer with more taste than gifts, but he certainly knew how to decorate a cocktail party. The terrace overlooking Central Park West was a garden of lovely women. Ah, but the one in blue.

"Who is she?" Hampton demanded, idly stirring his drink.

Stern appraised Tina. "Very nice piece. Not your type, though."

"Let me be the judge."

Stern shrugged. "Her name is Valentina Corvo."

"Exotic."

"She's a model, off-Broadway actress. Not a big name, but her face is starting to get around. It just made a *Mademoiselle* cover."

"European?"

"Fooled you. Just a nice little Sicilian-American from the Lower East Side. Rumors of Mafia connections."

"A peasant girl, I knew it. An introduction please."

Stern raised an eyebrow. "You gave Chloe her walking papers just this afternoon. Don't you think you ought to wait a respectful interim?"

"The divorce became legal today, but the split happened years ago, you know that Richard. The introduction."

Stella tut-tutted. "Why should I run interference for the opposition?" He cast another admiring glance at Tina. "I myself was thinking . . . "

Hampton grinned unkindly at his hermaphroditic friend. "She's certainly not your type, now is she? The introduction please."

Her handshake was warm and satiny. Her earthy vitality made his ex-wife, with all her breeding, look like a mule. Nick smiled his easy millionaire's smile, making artful small talk while the eye took open inventory. How nice. How very nice. Alluring combination of voluptuous breasts, small waist, wide hips, slender legs. He *had* to have this woman.

So began the brief mating of Nick Hampton and Valentina Corvo.

She of course had been mesmerized by his blond good looks, the romantic eyepatch, the big bank accounts. It had been so easy to ricochet right into his arms.

They honeymooned in Marrakech, slalomed on the Atlas slopes; high on kief they explored the Sahara in a Land Rover. Time froze.

Something about his bed manner had always made her feel uneasy though. But she wanted to believe in the fantasy lover, so at first she shelved her misgivings. When they returned to New York, the spell quickly dissolved.

His practiced hands worked wonders that left her oddly cold. At first she participated, exhibiting her own skills at body sorcercy. Tina was never the untouchable Sicilian maid, more the village *putana*, flaunting her hips and power in the *piazza*. So she was as proficient as Hampton. But soon she grew apathetic, then contemptuous. One night, after his slick-muscled body slid off, she whispered a complaint. "You're too rough. And your fuse is too short. Trouble is, Nick, you're all wrapped up in yourself. You're an efficient lover, all right. But you're like Narcissus in the sack."

"You find me inadequate?"

"Yup."

"How inspiring," he said coolly.

It was the beginning of the end.

Once she had made up her mind, Tina shrugged off doubt and self-reproach. Requisite youthful mistake. It was time to accept a truth that had always lurked in ambush, a sad realization since he was married with a baby on the way: Don Remo Santangelo was the only man who could make an honest woman of her. She packed her bags and left Hampton.

Still, she had been resigned to unhappiness. She knew that Ray too had made a bad marriage, but the child would give it mortar, longevity. Then the baby died.

Briefly she tasted remorse. Had she put some old country curse on the innocent child? Then she spat out the guilt, like chicory. She couldn't possibly be Nemesis to the man she loved, not she. To a rival she would show no quarter, but to Ray Santangelo? Her strong knees trembled at the thought of him. He would come to her.

And Remo finally came, dispirited, haunted like his namesake, in need of her restorative arts. In blushing triumph, she fell to the job, Valentina Corvo doing what came naturally. She was nursing him through the death of Arturo too, when all this started. She raked her ex-husband with her eyes, the bloodless mannequin on her corduroy couch.

The steel of the revolver felt cool in Hampton's flaming lap. Would he finally get to play out his fantasy? His tongue flickered over parched lips. This Sicilian girl still put the torch to him. He looked at her lush body. Why, dammit, did the old wop lady have to be around?

The idea had first come to him a week after Tina left him, after it had sunk in: *no Tina to play games with anymore.* His sexual interest in her still raged—how unusually bereft he felt. He knew his lust would die out in time, but he wasn't ready yet.

For a while, he bought expensive whores, but that didn't work.

The night he found even a thirteen-year-old Brazilian halfbreed prosaic and was showing her the door, it came to him. *Rape.* He wanted to rape Valentina.

Now frustration became foreplay. He began following her, using Hollywood cloak-and-dagger techniques—hat, trenchcoat, newspaper—he tracked her everywhere. Patiently he staked out the loft, the dance teacher, the topless bar. It was working already, he exulted in bed alone one night, hand pumping the last warm drop onto his flat belly.

Then Ray arrived on the scene. Hampton was in the Greek diner across the street as he saw them coming out of the Lolita Lounge together. Was this the neighborhood boyfriend she'd told him about the night they snorted coke in Sun Valley? Fits the description. Fine. It doubled the stakes, heightened the thrill. He trailed them to the loft, and waited until it was clear they were spending the night together. Then he huddled into his flannel-lined collar and hailed a cab.

By the time he closed his apartment door behind him, he had a tremendous hard-on. As he hung his keychain on a wrought-iron trivet in the vestibule he puzzled over which porno tape to put on the television in his bedroom. Perhaps a vintage piece, the 1934 dentist scene . . .

The separation agreement he had instructed his lawyer to prepare provided the excuse for a closer look in the morning. What he saw—the two of them still tingling in the aftermath—

firmed up his resolution. It would be a pleasure to violate such a man's Sicilian soulmate.

So it came as a shock to Hampton when they dropped out of sight even for a day. Had they left town? He started following Minnie, but soon got impatient. The old lady's comings and goings, strange as they were, told him nothing about Tina. He decided to take the ivory-handled Colt .45 from his late father's gun collection.

Valentina's loft had been easy to break into. The downstairs door was open, the upstairs lock a cinch to jimmy. All it took was his Swiss Army knife and ingenuity to put him where he now sat, pointing the gun at two women. But his scheme had gone awry. He had been counting on the law's reluctance to prosecute a husband for raping his wife, without corroboration of the act. But Minnie's presence spoiled everything. He lit another Turkish cigarette, holding it tightly in his mouth as if to compensate for his weakening resolution. This was more than he had bargained for.

Minnie caught his hesitation. At the very moment this man wavered and postured with a gun, life was almost surely being sapped from her son. As the headache hammered on, she wracked her brains for a way out. Then, "I'm leaving this place," she announced firmly. "I have to go to my son." Gruffly determined, she rose.

He leveled the gun, "Don't try it."

Minnie stopped, fists clenched. She looked at Tina, whose own gaze was fastened on the man holding the pistol.

How had she ever picked that rabbit for a husband? "It's me you want," she said, her voice gravelly with hatred. "Let this woman go."

He shook his head. "No way. Too late now." He peered down the gun barrel, dragging thoughtfully on the black cigarette.

Minnie focused on the eyepatch somewhere above the cigarette. She thought: he's outnumbered, four eyes to one. A vision of her feverish son flashed. She must act.

Holding her head in her hands, Minnie groaned operatically.

"What's the matter with her?" he asked suspiciously.

"Sick as a dog, poor thing," answered Tina, swooping down on her knees at Minnie's side, brushing back ringlets from her hot forehead. "I promised her a drink, to revive her kinda." Tina rose and made to go to the kitchen.

He stiffened. "Stay right there," he barked.

"Look," she pleaded. "She's a sick old lady and there's a bottle of scotch in the pantry. You can see into the kitchen from here."

After a moment's hesitation, Nick yielded with a nod.

Tiny moved toward the kitchen, her walk blatantly suggestive. Aware of her powers of distraction, she knew his Cyclops gaze would be nervously shifting from her hips to Minnie's groaning form. Tina didn't expect it would take very long.

Hampton was getting jumpy. Should he kill the old woman before raping Val? Police always suspected the estranged husband in such affairs. Maybe he could cover it up to look like a Sicilian family vendetta—religious Italian mamma fails to appreciate married altar-boy son bedding down topless barmaid; argument starts, tempers boil; barmaid picks up gun belonging to ex-husband, shoots Italian mamma; turns gun on self. It just might work.

Minnie was watching too. *Take the bull by the horns, rush him? Somebody might get hurt. Better to distract him, then go for the Achilles heel.*

Tina returned and fed Minnie the scotch. After the liquor had burned a trail down her throat, she said abruptly in Italian, "When I cry out, kick him in the balls."

Tina shot her a look of mingled admiration and shock.

Hampton snapped, "What did she say?"

"She said her head hurts," replied Tina.

Suddenly Minnie screamed shrilly and pointed a shaking finger toward his blind side.

Anthony Mancini

As he quickly whirled, Tina launched her muscled foot. The breath was vacuumed from him.

Minnie sank her teeth into the hand holding the gun. It clattered to the floor just as he managed a bellow of pain and outrage.

Tina retrieved the pistol.

Blood flowed over Nick's knuckles. His enraged glare vanished in the face of the scowling gun barrel. Tina had a firm grip. "Move an inch, I shoot."

He slumped back on the couch.

"I'll take care of him," she instructed Minnie. "You take care of that murderous witch."

Indecision flickered on Minnie's face.

"Get going. If you can't operate the elevator, take the stairs."

Minnie ran to the elevator, managed to slide shut the ponderous door, made the sign of the cross, and grabbed the lever.

Chapter 30

In a cheery room with hanging plants and a corner window view of the Corinthian façade of City Hall, Aunt Angela stared with an ancient, implacable hatred at Remo Santangelo's chalky, sleeping face.

The beam of envy would penetrate tonight, and it would be finished by daybreak. Through the son, she would destroy the white witch of the Abruzzi. Piece by piece.

She glanced at the illumined clock on the City Hall cupola. One-forty. Minnie's shift didn't begin until four. There was plenty of time to discharge her store of *invidia,* of venomous envy, of hatred stockpiled over years. Plenty of time.

Minnie used to have everything Angela had ever wanted: a rare gem of a devoted husband, a handsome son, a healthy grandson, *everything.* Soon she too would be void like Angela, barren as a tree in winter. Angela's green eyes burned bright.

Ray made a guttural sound in his sleep.

Once Angela too had had much to boast about—fair skin, curly hair, comfort, servants, a young husband, and a baby in the oven. Only the fair skin remained, a mask for her hatred and envy.

Perhaps her surroundings in Italy had not been especially grand, but at least there she lived in a finer state than her neighbors. On Thompson Street, my God, she lived like the rabble—like a dweller in the cavernous slums of Naples.

But nothing sickened her as much as the sight of Minnie's pious face, her lively eyes vibrating goodness. The hatred had been hard to contain all these years. Now the dam had burst.

She stabbed the young man with her gaze. Son of a conceited saint! Angela would humble her, make her taste bitter losses. Arturo too had been distracted by Minnie's gentle powers, her charming ways. She, with her beneficent magic, never lacked love. Now she could go to blazes along with her friend Arturo.

But not before she saw her own son in a coffin.

Angela heard the rumble of a delivery truck outside, bucking the cobblestoned streets of the financial district. To the north, City Hall slept soundly like a weary bureaucrat. A nurse laughed softly in the corridor, the sound mingling with Ray's uneven breathing.

Arturo. Killing him couldn't have been avoided. Not the way he had interfered, arming his friend Minnie with knowledge of the Old Ways, rousing her slumbering might. She killed him in a crude, simple way.

She had gone to his apartment on the pretense of stopping him from filling her cousin Minnie's head with nonsense about *malocchio*, leading her down primordial goatpaths. He opened the door with a knowing smile—obviously he had been expecting her.

She started scolding him, but he interrupted. "I know why you're here," he announced with a wan smile. "There's no need to pretend anymore."

She continued to feign ignorance. "Jesus, Joseph and Mary

what are you talking about?" She put down her tote bag and sat down on his cluttered couch.

"Do you invoke the saints?" he asked, shaking his head sorrowfully.

Her eyes grew smoky and she fell silent. The stuffed owl reproached her with his own hard, affronted gaze. She produced needles and yarn from her bag and began to knit. "You talk like a fool, Arturo," she said calmly. She touched the side of her head, making a screwing motion with her index finger. "Not quite right here." She cast down her eyes, returning to her knitting.

His smile was steady. *"Beware the three bridges,"* he said evenly.

She glared at him, her eyes jade. "What do you mean?" she demanded.

"You are the witch." Calmly lighting a cigar, he moved toward the door to the bedroom.

"Pah." She spat her fake disbelief.

"You overlooked the child."

She knitted.

"You praised him to the skies—you brought the peacock feathers to the baptism. I should have known. Juno's eyes. I should have known."

"I deny it," she insisted.

"You have the *malocchio*, envy in your eyes like poison in the glands of a snake."

"It's not true."

He opened the door to the bedroom, pausing weightily. "Then come inside."

She lay down the knitting and drew herself back. "In there? Why?"

"You have nothing to fear if you're innocent."

She stiffened. "Fear? What's in there?"

"Come and see."

"More mumbo jumbo."

"Are you afraid?"

"Don't be ridiculous, Arturo. What have I got to be afraid of, anyway?"

"Then come."

He opened the door wider as she hesitantly rose from the tattered couch. The dimly lit room yawned before her. He stepped inside and waited by the door. Carrying her knitting, she took short, faltering steps; then drew herself up proudly and entered.

Garlic, rue, and juniper assailed her nostrils. Wolves, boars, dogs, and dragons showed their gleaming teeth. Amulets discharged countervailing emanations, stinging her maleficent eyes. She recoiled, smarling like a cornered rat.

Arturo stood by the door, smiling. *"Strega,"* he accused.

She held her pounding head, then steeled herself. She looked at him. *"Porco,"* she shouted.

"Strega," he repeated calmly.

Without warning, she attacked, plunging the knitting needle straight into his right eye. He made a long, low, gurgling sound. Before he fell to the floor, she spent her cold fury by piercing his left eye as the veil of death descended over him. His body slumped to the floor.

She breathed heavily, her fat cheeks flushed, her hand shaking for a moment. Then she steadied herself and methodically finished the task.

Angela recalled the event with neither satisfaction nor remorse. Her eyes glowed like torches in the dark hospital room. Ray's death would be slower and even more painful. Angela was determined to extinguish his life by inches.

Not if Minnie could help it. She had slipped into the hospital room and was sitting in the dark by the other bed, with a view of her enemy outlined against the dome of City Hall, its statue holding high the scales of justice. She broke the silence, demanding through clenched teeth, "Take your filthy eyes off my son."

Angela swiveled her head in surprise.

The two women glared at each other like cats in a dark alley.

"So you know," Angela said without emotion.

"You witch."

Angela let out a chiming laugh, bringing Minnie's blood to a high boil, but she checked herself for the moment.

"You are a witch yourself," Angela said.

Minnie looked hard at the apostate. "What right did you have to kill Arturo?"

"He was old. He was useless."

Minnie's mouth curled with loathing. "He was a good man. You killed him cruelly, like an animal."

"We are all animals. You're a she-goat from the barbarous mountains of Abruzzi. I'm a she-wolf from the border of Lucania. We are what we are, it was ordained long ago."

"We are natural enemies," said Minnie, rising from the chair and approaching her adversary. Moonlight bathed Minnie's face. "You robbed Arturo of his last years. You put out the light of his good eyes, brutally . . . wantonly . . ."

"I hate you," Angela said.

"When I think of what you did to Arturo," continued Minnie, "I think of the code of Hammurabi, the law of Babilonia."

Angela smirked complacently. "You won't get my eyes."

"An eye for an eye, two eyes for two eyes."

Angela waggled her shoulders. "You haven't the guts, Minnie Santangelo."

Minnie ground her teeth. "The guts I have, the cruelty I don't. But I will win. Your eyes will never again touch my son." Her voice boomed in the quiet room, "And what about my grandson, you pig of Satan? You were his *godmother!*"

"The devil took him."

Minnie punched her with all her force, square in the teeth, knocking her off the chair. "Just because *you* say your rosaries to him doesn't make him king of the world. My pure grandson went to God. And you better get that straight or I *will* pluck your eyes out."

Angela gingerly felt around her mouth. "You'll pay for that."

"What's going on here?"

The night nurses' supervisor was a big black woman with sable skin and the bearing of a military governor. She peered through horn rims at the scene: Minnie with fists on hips, standing over Angela bleeding from the mouth. "Are you ladies nuts? This is a hospital with sick people, not a barroom." Her face gleamed like hard ebony. "Now you haul ass and take your hassle out to the street where it belongs."

Angela struggled to her feet, still rubbing her mouth. "She hit me. What about my lip?"

The nurse roughly lifted Angela's chin and inspected the damage. "It's just a split lip. You won't die of it. Now haul ass, I said."

Minnie was calm. "Just a little family argument, you understand." She grabbed Angela by the shoulder. "Come on, we'll patch it up over a cup of coffee.

Angela glared at Minnie, then turned to the nurse. "I want to stay here. My nephew needs me."

The nurse's hand shot out from her side, pointed to the door. "Out—or I call a cop."

Minnie darted to her son's side, placing a cheek to his. The breathing was steady. Weeping, she kissed his stubbled cheek. *"Corraggio,* Ray. Mamma will take care of everything."

By the time they had reached the elevator, Angela's lip was puffed up and she was dabbing at it with an embroidered handkerchief. Somewhere on the hospital-room floor lay two of her teeth.

"We'll finish this outside," said Minnie.

"I won't run away," said Angela.

The automatic doors parted and the women walked erectly through the lobby, with its potted plants and picture window, toward the William Street exit.

The night tingled with cold as they walked through the parking lot toward Beekman Street, a canyon under the towering buildings of the Wall Street district. The sound of their footsteps echoed amid the shuttered stores and restaurants. The only light shone in a fire house next door to the blue awning of the Wall Street synagogue. An occasional car or delivery van rattled over the cobblestoned streets.

They stopped in front of Max's Swiss Chalet, directly under the old pendant sign. They eyed each other threateningly, neither flinching from the inevitable encounter.

Angela, planting her plump legs wide, filled her lungs with cold air. She had her back toward the restaurant's front window, a large pane rimmed by stained-glass panels. Behind the picture window, amber lights picked out green plants and a pitted stone cherub pouring water from a jardiniere. Angela's shoulders rose and fell rhythmically.

Minnie, proud as a samurai, stood with arms folded and her back to the street. Two trees, potted in barrels on the sidewalk, flanked her. "My son will live," she announced.

Angela laughed derisively, baring teeth large and sharp as a swine's. She raised a taloned hand to her mouth and sniggered, fat flesh quivering under the gaslight fixture. She composed herself.

"I had a son once," she said with an air of disclosure. "He didn't live."

Minnie smiled maliciously. "But he *does* live."

Angela pouted grotesquely. "I never had a son. I was lying to you."

Minnie's tone was even. "He lives."

Under the light, Angela's face was livid with hatred, then drained of color. "You lie."

"You know him, in fact," Minnie continued. "He's a neighbor."

The lamp sparkled on Angela's hair, and her crowning glory as a girl in Montevecchio now resembled a nest of wriggling snakes. "You lie, lie, lie, you whore."

Minnie was relentless. "They lied when they told you he

was dead. They gave him away to Eva and sent them both away to America. *Here*—to Little Italy."

A brute hiss came from deep in her throat. "Don't say another word." Her bulging eyes seemed near popping "I'll kill you. I'll petrify you, Minerva Santangelo."

Minnie kept speaking calmly. "Eva became a nun, you know, Angela. And the boy grew up, in a manner of speaking. Would you like to see him?"

Angela's long nails dug into her palms. "No," she replied hoarsely.

"Where is your mother love?" Minnie asked innocently.

"I'll destroy you," Angela hissed.

Minnie turned her glance to the right. "You are far more ugly than he." The sound of shuffling steps broke the silence of the narrow streets.

Refusing to look, Angela fastened her eyes on Minnie who continued the taunting monologue: "Don't you want to see him? He has joined us on this enchanting night."

Angela scowled. "You'll be sorry you were born."

Minnie's hand pointed down the street with the authority and power of a flaming sword. "Gaze on your own reflection, monster."

Angela turned around.

The street lamp spotlit the little man in the white shirt and windbreaker, shambling toward them. Angela look horrified, then turned her hot eyes on Minnie. "Is this your Perseus?" she asked drily. "Is your hero a hunchback?"

Minnie responded with a radiant smile.

The *strega* turned back to Fortunato. "Get outta here, *gobbo*. This is none of your business."

Mock tenderness lit his face as he extended a stubby hand. "Mamma."

Angela shielded her face with an arm. "Go to hell," she screamed down the vaulted, echoing streets. "Or I will send you there. Go back where you came from."

"I came from you."

Minnie Santangelo and the Evil Eye

"You lie." The eyes blazed like bonfires. "Lie through your rotten teeth."

"Don't be ashamed of me, Mamma. He chuckled. "When I learned you were my mother, I came on winged feet."

He approached her shivering form.

Angela rattled her snaky head. "I'll squash you like a beetle."

Now Minnie stepped between them, planting her feet firmly on the sidewalk.

"Squash me first."

The stone figures adorning the surrounding municipal buildings stood silent witness as the witches locked eyes. Under the satyr smile of the petrified cherub in the restaurant window, they stared mightily at each other until the headache struck at Minnie with near blinding force, bringing her to the brink of collapse. She leaned against a tree trunk, struggling to keep her feet, squeezing her eyes open and shut. Then the good witch remembered what she had in the pocket of her cardigan.

Her hand found the coral horn, the amulet Cynthia had removed from the baby's neck. Just holding it helped renew her strength. She regained her proud posture and stared the furious *strega* down, then took out the horn and displayed it.

Angela seethed. This stubborn *strega benevola* would not give way. She heard the truck clattering up the stony streets and immediately decided on drastic measures.

The driver of the *Daily News* delivery van whistled and flipped the steering wheel left for the turn onto William Street. As he cleared the narrow corner, he stepped down hard on the gas pedal. Everything seemed to happen at once. Angela made a savage lunge at Minnie, but Fortunato broke the force of the *strega's* attack with a growling butt to the stomach, sending her hurtling backward toward the plate-glass window.

The driver's eyes widened as the unexpected form hurtled into his path. He swerved and his wheels missed Minnie's body by half a foot.

Anthony Mancini

Glass showered the sidewalk. After a silent second, a burglar alarm sounded.

Minnie dusted herself off and quickly went to Fortunato's side. He stood unharmed amid the shards of glass near the broken window, staring dumbly at his mother's body.

The driver, who had run his front wheels up on the opposite sidewalk, walked over to them. "Jesus, what's going on?"

Minnie looked into the broken window at the cherub, starting with its smile, tracing to the hand tilting the water jar. The jar was poised above the dishevelled ringlets of hair spangled with bits of glass. Minnie turned away, retching.

Angela Treponti had been decapitated.

Christmas Eve

Christmas Eve came to the urban village. The Mott Street record store played "Silver Bells" over the loudspeaker and everybody went to see the manger scene, big as life, that the friars had set up in front of Saint Anthony's. Delicious aromas poured from the tenement kitchens into the neighborhood where cold weather helped quell the rival smells of garbage.

On Hester Street, Minnie Santangelo assembled the vigil meal: spaghetti in fish sauce; roast sausage, hot and sweet; and a big salad crowded with mushrooms, capers, sharp cheeses, and anchovies. She picked flakes of pasta dough from her stubby fingers and hummed a Nativity song, remembering the shepherd's pipes of her homeland. *"Tu scendi dalle stelle, O Re del cielo,"* she sang. "You come down from the stars, O King of heaven."

In the living room of the railroad apartment, Ray smiled with satisfaction. He smoked a pipe while shaving with an electric razor and watching basketball on the TV. Minnie was her old self again, he thought. She'd even gone back to playing bingo.

He wasn't faring badly himself, Ray reflected as he bit his lower lip to stretch the skin below it for the razor. He had finally won the battle with the illness, whatever it was.

Encephalitis, the doctors had said. "Speculated" was a better word. The bug disappeared as mysteriously as it had come. And if his brain had indeed been on fire, the damage wasn't noticeable. He smiled to himself: at least not yet. Who knew? Maybe it *was* the evil eye, after all. At halftime, he went to the kitchen.

"Smells fantastic in here," he said, trying to sneak a sliver of spaghetti dough.

She hit his wrist with a wooden spoon. "That's enough," she scolded, secretly delighted at the resurgence of his appetite.

"When do we eat? I need something to tide me over."

She applied a rolling pin to the dough. "They should all be here in no time. Sit, keep me company."

He pulled a wooden chair up to the kitchen table and sat backwards on it, watching her work. "I got about ten minutes until the second half." After a pause, he said, "I'm glad we're celebrating Christmas."

"We can't beat our breasts forever," she replied, hauling the *chitarra,* down from a shelf.

"Yeah," he agreed. "We have mourned enough."

"After all, we have things to be thankful for."

He nodded silently in agreement.

"Have you heard from Cynthia?"

He shook his head. "But her mother wrote again. She was released from the hospital and has gone to live in the country somewhere. She asked her mother to ask me for a divorce."

Minnie grimaced sympathetically. "It was never a marriage, not a real marriage."

Emotion colored his cheeks. "Suppose not."

"I know it's hard."

He cracked a smile. "It's better this way."

"Is she over her illness?"

He went to the refrigerator for a bottle of beer. "Her mother says she's a little better. I hope it's true." He sat down again, poured the malty liquid into a glass decorated with a Mickey Mouse decal, and took a long deep swallow.

Minnie could see through the kitchen window the sign identifying Hester Street in black letters over a yellow background. Snowflakes swirled in the nimbus of the street lamp and fell to drape a clean mantle of white on the mottled asphalt. Holiday lights flickered behind fire escapes and Santa Claus effigies leered like Bacchuses behind the store windows. The scene fit her present outlook: a few bright spots in a gloomy terrain.

Not unexpectedly, the Medusan encounter had haunted Minnie's nights. But now the incubi were beginning to slip away. Optimism, indomitable in Minnie, reasserted itself.

One thing for sure: she lost no sleep over the fate of Angela. She had had it coming to her.

Doctor Bevilaqua arrived with his Irish wife, a woman whose hair and speech were clipped, an ascetic type, rarefied like mountain air. Though poles apart in personality, she and Minnie hit it off.

Mrs. Bevilaqua bowed with distant formality, like a Tibetan monk, while Minnie and Ray responded in effusive welcome.

"Will somebody take these off my hands?" asked the doctor gruffly.

"You shouldn't have brought anything," Minnie said with more than reflex courtesy, while Ray took the pile of gaily wrapped packages and put them under a white artificial Christmas tree.

Bevilaqua ignored her. "When do we eat?"

"Have a drink," Minnie urged, "while we wait for the others. Everything's practically ready. Have a glass of wine, maybe a Campari."

"I took care of that too," said Bcvliaqua, producing a bottle from the inside pocket of his topcoat. "Vernaccia."

"What is it?" Minnie asked, rounding up four glasses, ready to drink no matter.

Bevilaqua looked sheepishly at his wife before answering.

"A wine from Sardinia. Goes great with fish and fish sauces."

"I'll just have mineral water, if you don't mind," said Mrs. Bevilaqua, smiling benignly. "But please enjoy yourselves."

The doctor sighed resignedly as he popped the cork. "East is east and west is west," he said. He poured.

"Oooh, it's so beautiful—so green," said Minnie.

Bevilaqua nodded. "Like Brazilian wine."

Ray smiled somewhat perversely. "Green like envy."

The group fell silent. Bevilaqua frowned at any reference, oblique or otherwise, to the *malocchio*. "Green as grapes," he said, taking a drink.

Ray gave in to an impish impulse. "Green as snakes, did you say?" he asked, drinking too.

"You know very well what I said," the doctor insisted. He looked at Minnie who was pouring mineral water for his wife. "Drink up," he said. "It's very good wine."

But Ray's joke had already succeeded in conjuring up in Bevilaqua's memory the picture of Angela's severed head as he had seen it that night in the restaurant window, a grotesquely compelling verd-antique of the snaky-haired angel, rusty with blood. In his years as a coroner's gumshoe in the Medical Examiner's office, he had seen many decapitations, especially in subway accidents or suicides. But he'd never before seen a beheading quite so . . . esthetic. It was the only way he could put it.

The blade of the guillotine had been an especially large shard in the cascade of plate glass that fell in the restaurant window where soft artificial light, greenery and objets d'art played prettily against the grisly head. The tableau glowed like amber in his memory.

Soon Father Mancuso arrived to poke his mournful face into the conversation, mistakenly assuming the topic was wine. "I've never tried Vernaccia," the priest confessed, holding out a glass. He licked his lips before drinking.

Now came Fortunato with a box of eclairs and cannoli from Borgia's Bakery to add to the array of desserts. He wore a tie and new sport jacket over his customary white shirt. Minnie, who had half-expected him not to show up, greeted him with obvious delight.

Sister Anastasia had not been invited. She drank more and more by herself nowadays and wouldn't have accepted anyway. Fortunato was still church caretaker but did his best to avoid his foster mother since the night she had explained the riddle of the three bridges, the secret of his origins.

He had fled the convent slavering like a rabid dog for revenge, leaving Minnie and the nun in the parlor. The door to Angela's apartment had trembled under his pounding fist. No answer. Muscular legs carried him over the sidewalks and streets, through the stores and social clubs until he finally traced her to the hospital, then to the silent arena in front of Willy's Restaurant.

The police had wanted to pin a manslaughter rap on him but couldn't make it stick. The dwarf's insistence to the Legal Aid lawyer that he was guilty of "matricide" didn't impress the judge who dismissed the charges.

The detectives were equally skeptical when Minnie told them that Fortunato had accidentally killed Angela in an effort to save her own life, especially since Minnie refused to explain the motive for the fight. But they couldn't prove otherwise.

Fortunato had come through his night of trial feeling oddly peaceful, almost like a demi-demigod for once ready to pluck his share of golden apples. Tonight he even accepted Minnie's offer of a glass of wine.

Valentina arrived late, wearing a fur-trimmed Cossack coat and eyebrows penciled severely—mock Art Deco. Minnie smiled to herself as she noticed Ray's eyes light up at her appearance. Cooing like a pigeon, Bevilaqua helped Tina off with her bulky coat. He was an old votary of the female form.

She and Minnie embraced enthusiastically.

"*Buon Natale*, Signora," she said, emotion warming her delicate face. "Merry Christmas." Then she pouted. "I had a present for you, a big bottle of expensive perfume." Her face fell another inch. "But I left it in the taxi."

Minnie shrugged good-naturedly. "So I'll smell like garlic. Is that so bad? Have a drink and forget it."

Frowning, Ray draped an arm over Tina's shoulder. "Where's *my* Merry Christmas?"

Tina patted his behind and pecked him on the cheek. "Go get us a drink."

His mouth turned down. "What'll it be?" he said in defeat.

"Scotch," commanded Minnie. She would celebrate with stronger stuff than usual.

Smiling, Tina made a proud appraisal of her. "You should be Minnie Buonocchio, with your good eye. Ah, what a *nonnetta* you'll make!"

Minnie's cheer fled momentarily, under the onslaught of recent memories. She chewed her lip and looked down at her own rough hands. "I'm not always proud of what happened."

"I won't hear any of it. You did nothing to be ashamed of. She got a dose of her own medicine, and that's that."

Minnie gazed at her, blinking with gratitude. Then she said coldly. "Yes, she killed the baby, didn't she? And murdered Arturo. But she died so horribly."

"As she lived."

Minnie now looked intently into space, motionless, diligently trying to plumb the mysteries of what had happened. Suddenly she shivered. "Was it all really the way we think it was? Did she really have the evil eye? Do you believe in it, Tina?"

"Believe in what?" asked Ray, handing them their drinks.

"Santa Claus," said Tina. "Why don't you go discuss ancient history with Bevilaqua?"

Light dawned on his handsome face. "I see. Girl talk." Good-natured crows' feet appeared at the corners of his gray eyes before he turned on his heel to seek out the learned doctor.

Minnie looked around conspiratorily. "He hasn't ever tried to bother you again, has he?"

"Nah," said Tina, after taking a slug of scotch. "Not since I let him go with a warning. I think the bastard has enough of Sicilian women."

"I'm not Sicilian."

"You know what I mean."

"If Ray ever found out . . ."

"I know. He'd do something violent."

"And end up in jail, or worse. He's still your husband, after all."

Tina grimaced. "For about two more weeks. Least, that's what my lawyer says. We could file a complaint and prosecute."

"Who would believe it?"

"You're right. They'd only tag us as a couple of hot-blooded Latin ladies. That dapper lawyer of his would package him up real pretty for the judge."

"Okay then, we let it lie." Minnie studied the young woman, measured her from head to foot. "So what are you—a good witch or a bad witch?"

"No witch at all, I'm afraid," Tina smiled.

Minnie frowned. "Modesty does not become you. You got the makings, you know."

Through the drafty windows, they could hear carols playing on the record-store loudspeaker, plucking old music from the same heartstring as their rough-hewn ancestors, those human beings crafted like their work from the very best of material and with the greatest of skill. The God of Minnie and Tina and of people like them was indeed a master Maker.

"I got a present for you, you know," Minnie said.

Tina looked delighted. "Wonderful. Where is it?"

"It's too good to wrap." Minnie took her hands in hers. "I'm going to give you the power."

"I thought you had to be born with it."

"You were born with the tendency, inherited from your grandmother. The power is passed along on Christmas Eve."

"What a gift!"

Anthony Mancini

Minnie doused her forefinger with olive oil from a quart can and crossed Tina's forehead. "A sign is needed. The rules are not in any book, really. But you'll know them." Her hand fell heavily to her side. "Noble grace is passed along through strong families, I believe."

Tina took another drink, then wiped her mouth with exuberance. Suddenly, she frowned. "I'm so sorry I lost your present."

"I told you not to worry." A tear welled in Minnie's mighty eye. "I got the best Christmas gift of all, you know. I have a family again."

And they interlocked eyes as they toasted each other with scotch, touching glasses in a run-down tenement on one of the anarchic streets of Little Italy.